THE NEW KID

M A V I S   J U K E S

Alfred A. Knopf New York

THIS IS A BORZOI BOOK PUBLISHED BY ALFRED A. KNOPF

Visit us on the Web! randomhouse.com/kids

Educators and librarians, for a variety of teaching tools,
visit us at randomhouse.com/teachers

Library of Congress Cataloging-in-Publication Data
Jukes, Mavis.
The new kid / by Mavis Jukes.
p. cm.
Summary: When almost-nine-year-old Carson Blum and his father move to Northern California, he is worried about adjusting to his new, large public school and finding friends.
ISBN 978-0-375-85879-6 (trade) — ISBN 978-0-375-95879-3 (lib. bdg.) —
ISBN 978-0-375-89631-6 (ebook)
[1. Moving, Household—Fiction. 2. Schools—Fiction. 3. Friendship—Fiction.
4. Single-parent families—Fiction.] 1. Title.
PZ7.J9294Ne 2011
[Fic]—dc22
2010048826

The text of this book is set in 13.5-point Goudy Old Style.

Printed in the United States of America
December 2011
10 9 8 7 6 5 4 3 2 1

First Edition

To the memory of Marguerite Jukes—
a legendary teacher, a great mom, a great
grandma, and a great great-grandma.

PROLOGUE
The Plan

Carson would be moving before the school year ended, from a very small private Montessori school where he knew everybody to a very huge public elementary school where he knew nobody.

Carson would be the New Kid.

And that was something he'd never been before.

His dad had been offered a new position in a different area. His decision to change office locations had been a difficult one. He would make a better salary, and be given more interesting assignments. Plus, he could name his hours, and sometimes work from his computer at home. Best yet, he could spend more time with Carson, and drive him to school each morning, and pick him up each afternoon. Being able to spend more time with Carson had been the tipping point. He accepted the offer.

Changing jobs and schools is never easy, but everything is easier once you have a plan, and this was the plan they made together:

Carson, Genevieve, their Labrador, and Moose would stay at Carson's grandparents while his dad got established up north in El Cerrito, California.

At Carson's grandparents' house, Genevieve would carry rocks around in the backyard. Evenings they would walk her with the nose leash over to the neighborhood park, where she would bark at birds. At night, after Bird Patrol was over and done with, she'd doze on her blankie in her basket by the back door and guard her toys and food dish.

Moose would sit tight and cool his hooves on Carson's bedspread. At night, he'd recline—with the backs of his two bald ears on the pillow, his eyes wide open, and his nose sticking up.

Carson didn't put it on the ten o'clock news that, at age going-on-nine, he slept next to a stuffed animal.

But he was planning to boot Moose out of the bed sometime before his next birthday. When Carson turned nine, it would be time to put Moose up on a shelf.

That wouldn't happen until after they moved.

Once Carson's dad had rented a house and super-vised the move on both ends, they would be ready to roll. They'd ferry the old classic orange Porsche up, and later on Carson's grandparents would bring up the other car, the station wagon, stay awhile, then fly back to Pasadena. That would happen on his grand-pa's vacation.

So yes. They had a plan, and the plan went off without a hitch.

1. GOOD-BYE,
Pasadena

Early one evening, when crickets were creaking and the smell of flowers was in the warm, damp air, Case and Gavin, Carson's two best friends, their families, and other friends and neighbors gathered, along with the teachers, at the Montessori school for a Good-Luck Potluck Farewell.

Everybody knew what Carson's favorite dinner was, and many families forgot to check the sign-up list, so there were eleven pans of lasagna and twenty-two loaves of garlic bread.

They all chipped in on a present for Carson and his dad: a croquet set in a carrying case. Carson's grandparents would bring it up in the station wagon, just in time for croquet games on sunny summer afternoons.

The morning after the Good-Luck Potluck Farewell, beneath a pastel peach Pasadena sunrise, Carson and his dad backed the orange Porsche out of the driveway onto the street. Grandma and Grandpa were standing on the front lawn, Grandpa's arm slung around Grandma's shoulder. If they were sad, they wouldn't have shown it. They lifted their coffee cups to say good-bye.

Carson's dad chose the scenic route. Genevieve sat with Moose in the front seat, and Carson sat in the back, in the jump seat. Actually, Genevieve sat *on* Moose in the front seat, but Moose didn't mind. Moose was a mellow guy. He couldn't see much scenery, but it was nice and warm under Genevieve.

Genevieve's suitcase was strapped onto the rear deck with bungee cords. In it were her dog dishes, kibble, blankie, and squeak toys. Most of the squeak toys didn't squeak anymore, but that didn't keep Genevieve from poking them with her nose or holding them in her mouth. She was holding a silent rubber ham in her mouth and looking out the window at a breathtakingly scenic stretch of long and lonesome highway when the engine sputtered and died.

Luckily, the cell phone worked way out there in the middle of nowhere, and they called for roadside assistance.

Half an hour passed before they saw the big blue and yellow tow truck come down the highway. Carson held Genevieve on her leash, and she sat like the good girl that she always tried to be, and sometimes really was.

It was dicey getting the Porsche onto the back of the flatbed truck. At one point, when the chains were rattling and clanging and the motor was grinding and whining, Carson's dad had to cover his face with his Porsche cap.

Carson and his dad and Genevieve and the tow-truck guy all rode crammed into the front seat of the cab as they headed to the nearest town. Carson sat buckled up in the middle, in front of an ashtray brimming with cigarette butts, ashes, and gray wads of chewing gum. Outside the window, the view was mighty nice.

They rumbled along, first next to a rocky stream with light dancing on the water. Then they chugged up through a canyon and into a grassy basin dotted with black cattle. Carson saw piney ridges and rocky hillsides, a silver river, and craggy, glacier-topped peaks against the backdrop of a clear, sunshiny blue sky.

Genevieve sat happily plopped on Carson's dad's lap, squashing him and blocking his view, her tongue hanging out—and her nose making smudges on the window. And her tail wagging every once in a while, with the tip bopping Carson on the ear.

Eventually, they came to a one-horse highway town. The tow-truck guy dropped the Porsche off at a tin garage with AUTOMOTIVE REPAIR and a picture of a gorilla painted on the front.

It was closed for the day.

Carson, Genevieve, and his dad walked over to the little old-timey Three Cowboys Motel. They were happy to see the sign that said WI-FI, CABLE TV, PETS WELCOME ON MANAGER'S APPROVAL. Carson unzipped his jacket and took Moose out. Outside the office, a creepy gnome with a chipped nose and fat cheeks was sitting with a family of plaster skunks in the grass.

Virgil, the motel owner, manager, handyman, and

maid, approved Genevieve and gave Carson's dad the Wi-Fi password, then his dad opened his laptop and located a website that shipped classic Porsche parts anywhere in the United States.

So that's where they stayed for three days, in the Three Cowboys Motel, waiting for a rebuilt fuel pump to be delivered by UPS.

They were traveling light. Good thing because the motel room was small.

Carson brought in his suitcase, which contained a change of clothes and his treasure box—a cookie tin containing Various Important Small Items, including his bottle-cap collection.

The motel room had twin beds, bent miniblinds, a dresser, and a small TV in a pine cupboard. The bathroom had three small bars of perfumed soap wrapped up in pale pink glossy paper on a glass shelf and a white metal shower stall with a pink plastic curtain.

A lock with a spiderweb in it could be adjusted to allow the window to be left open a crack, and Carson slid the window a couple of inches to counteract the boggy smell.

A cheery little lamp on the night table had horseshoes printed on the shade and a carved tipsy cowpoke on the base of it, dozing against a pole. Out the window, a blinking arrow pointed to MABEL'S FAMILY-STYLE CAFÉ, the town's one-and-only restaurant, located right next door. A bright red neon sign flashed EAT, EAT, EAT, EAT, EAT, EAT, and that's where they ate, ate, ate breakfast, lunch, and dinner.

Evenings Carson and his dad wandered out to stargaze in the meadow behind the motel. Genevieve came, too, and sat quietly with a yellow Frisbee in her mouth.

Carson looked up at the sky and wondered who he would meet at Valley Oak Elementary School that could be as good a friend as Gavin or Case.

Would anybody even like Carson?

Even a little bit?

He couldn't see why not.

But he'd have to wait to find out.

Carson's dad turned the delay into a photo op. They investigated a tumbledown old cabin.

"Can you believe people used to homestead places like this? Squatters' rights," his dad said.

He squatted down and pointed his camera right at a bumblebee that was bouncing and bumbling from flower to flower like a fat black and yellow ball. He zoomed in and clicked. The bumblebee zoomed up. And chased him into some mucky goop by a spring.

"You okay, Dad?" Carson called.

He was fine. Muddy pants, wet shoes. So what.

They strolled along the fence line behind the automotive repair shop where the Porsche was waiting to be fixed, now parked inside and all by itself except for a pack rat Carson spotted through the window. The pack rat was hiding behind an empty metal paint can—holding on to the edge and peering at them with beady black eyes and twitching its whiskers.

Carson didn't mind pack rats, but his dad wasn't a fan. He stared through the dusty pane, shook his head, and sighed deeply. "Wow. I didn't sign up for this."

Carson and his dad uploaded some landscape photos, a portrait of the gnome, and a close-up of the bumblebee onto the laptop and emailed them to Carson's grandma and grandpa, Case, Gavin, and Carson's Montessori teacher, Ms. Juli.

On the last evening, they each sat in front of a pile of Mabel's too-red spaghetti, which tasted like noodles dunked in ketchup. Carson sat by the window, where he could slyly part the checkered curtain to keep his sharp eye on the motel room, where Genevieve was sleeping.

His dad twirled some spaghetti in a spoon and grumbled, "I've had a bellyful of the scenic route, Carson." He sucked in one very long noodle.

"There's sauce on your chin, Dad."

"Thanks, son." He went on to say that he had once heard of a pack rat that nested in the engine compartment of a Porsche Speedster. "So before any fuzzy, flea-ridden, beady-eyed, bucktoothed rodent takes up residence in the Porsche," he told Carson, "I want to get us the heck outta Dodge!"

He stabbed the salad: iceberg lettuce with a big blob of bottled ranch dressing on top. He told Carson that, although he owned one of the greatest pairs of cowboy boots ever made by Dan Post, when it came to home on the range, home on the ranch, dude ranches, ranchettes, ranch dressing, or ranch anything else—no thanks. Home on the front porch of the sunny two-story house he had rented in El Cerrito—yes please, and the sooner the better.

"I thought you said you were giving those cowboy boots away because they pinch your toes," Carson told his dad.

"They do, but I couldn't part with them."

Carson took a bite of the garlic roll. Yum! He liked squishy white rolls, but his dad was critical of too-soft bread. His dad wasn't officially a restaurant critic, but he was a certified foodie. He had a blog: *Gourmet Grub*.

Mabel came around with a pot full of coffee the color of tea and asked how everything was, and Carson and his dad both said great! So she brought them a complimentary dessert: soggy corn flakes and granulated sugar on baked apple slices with whipped cream on top that she blasted out of a can. Carson liked it!

"How many stars would you give this place?" he whispered.

Carson's dad made a zero sign by touching his thumb to his pointing finger and peering at Carson through the circle. "But don't tell Mabel. She's a peach!"

He got up and dropped a few quarters in the jukebox and stared down at the selections. When his first song began to play, he stood with his hands on the jukebox, bopping to the music and jutting his chin in and out.

The next morning the part arrived. A tall mechanic with bright blue eyes and a bushy orange beard as big as a bird's nest installed the rebuilt fuel pump.

Off they went! Carson's dad shifted through the gears. To Carson, there was no place he'd rather be than driving with his dad through wide-open spaces— fast and low to the ground.

Except maybe heading back to Pasadena to plan a birthday barbecue with his family and friends.

Many hours later, Carson's dad announced, "Okay, son. We're almost home."

They drove down a two-lane highway, past a billboard for Atlas Speedway that said DEMOLITION DERBY and had a big picture of a bashed-up car splattered with mud. They came to the WELCOME TO EL CERRITO PLEASE DRIVE CAREFULLY sign, and drove carefully through the center of town. Then they turned into a residential neighborhood full of tree-lined streets that crossed each other.

"Get ready. We're really close now."

A moment later, they turned into the driveway of their spacious, gracious rented home, which had a big front porch and a garden full of flowering bushes.

Carson's dad shut off the engine and turned to Carson. "Like it?"

Was he kidding?

Carson loved it!

As much as he could have, under the circumstances of being the New Kid, with no friends in town.

2. HELLO,
El Cerrito

The first thing Genevieve wanted to do after her suitcase was unpacked was to investigate her new surroundings while holding a tennis ball in her mouth.

So, off they all went to Green Gulch Regional Park.

Green Gulch Regional Park wasn't a city park with trimmed bushes and pink cement paths and a fountain with a bronze dolphin spitting water in it, like the park in Pasadena. It was a wilder park.

At the northern entrance, there was a group campground in a meadow. A trail wound up through the redwoods, ending at a small amphitheater. They sat in on a talk about predatory birds, given by an enthusiastic park ranger wearing a green uniform and a brown flat-brimmed Smokey Bear hat with dents in the crown.

A hawk screeched from the treetop.

Carson's dad had to warn Genevieve, in a whisper: "No barking, stop it, I mean it!" several times.

When a flock of crows flew overhead, Genevieve went on High Bird Alert, and they decided to excuse themselves completely.

The southern entrance to the park was within walking distance of Carson's house and involved a large pond. Carson and his dad decided it would be wise to leave Genevieve at home to explore her new, spacious fenced backyard while they walked over to get acquainted with the ducks.

Five or six people sat in folding chairs staring at plastic fishing floats floating on the surface of the water. "Grandpa and Grandma would like to fish here, wouldn't they, Dad?"

"Yup."

"I'm really going to miss seeing them on my birthday."

"I will, too. But we'll see them soon afterward."

That cheered Carson up.

They walked to the other side and cheerily fed the ducks Cheerios—just a few. It wasn't exactly duck food, but judging by waddle speed and quack volume, they liked it a lot. So did the crows, who dipped down, landed, squawked, flapped their wings, marched around, stuck their tongues out at each other, and greedily gobbled up every O they could beat the ducks to.

Carson was quite the animal lover. But crows weren't exactly at the top of his list.

He did like horses. And he wanted to learn to ride one. Beyond the pond, past the public tennis courts, there was a corral and a big barn with a sign that said RED BARN STABLES: TRAIL RIDES AND WESTERN RIDING LESSONS. WELCOME, Y'ALL!

"Hmmm. I have an idea," his dad said. "How about for your birthday, we go on a trail ride! And you can bring a new friend! And your new friend can bring a parent to supervise."

Carson said, "If I don't have a new friend in time for my birthday, maybe just I could go and you could supervise me."

His dad put his arm around Carson's shoulder. "Don't worry, son. You'll have a new friend in time."

Suddenly, without any warning, Carson's heart sank like a stone. He couldn't imagine a birthday without his grandma and grandpa.

"You okay, Carson?"

"Sure I am, Dad."

As okay as he could be, under the circumstances of being about to become the lonesomest cowboy in Green Gulch Park.

On his first day of school, his dad took out his phone and photoed Carson standing in front of a sign that said VALLEY OAK ELEMENTARY SCHOOL with a bucktoothed squirrel holding an acorn carved into the wood.

Carson managed a smile.

In some ways, Valley Oak was a little bit different from Rainbow Ridge Montessori, but in most ways it was, well, completely and totally, utterly 100 percent different.

At Rainbow Ridge, kids wore clothes to school, like T-shirts and shorts or sweatshirts and jeans.

At Valley Oak, kids wore uniforms to school, like white shirts and tan pants or white shirts and tan pants. Or white shirts and tan skirts or white shirts and tan skirts. And various other garments and accessories with a Valley Oak logo embroidered on them: either a squirrel or an acorn. Carson opted for the acorn logo. He had a whole new set of clothes, and all were carefully marked *Carson B.* on the labels with a fine-tip permanent marker.

He had a brand-new white shirt and tan pants, a brand-new white shirt and tan pants, a brand-new Valley Oak zip-up hoodie with a silhouette of an acorn on the front, a brand-new Valley Oak jacket with a silhouette of an acorn on the sleeve, and a brand-new Valley Oak backpack with a silhouette of an acorn on the flap in the back.

Carson didn't have a brand-new Valley Oak beanie with a silhouette of an acorn on the side. Carson didn't wear hats with green pom-poms that looked like pesto piled on top.

Carson had to carry his brand-new acorn backpack back and forth to school, packed with homework and papers for his dad to sign and send back.

He would have liked a brand-new Valley Oak friend, who would one day become his good ol' Valley Oak old friend.

He hoped to be invited to play with one of the kids after school, but he hadn't.

Not yet.

He felt like the New Kid that he actually was. And he felt like he was on the outside of a circle, looking in.

Friends like Case and Gavin, well, you can't make those overnight.

Carson knew that.

The principal, Ms. Pierson, had placed Carson in Mr. Skip Lipman's class. Mr. Lipman seemed to be a good guy. And Carson saw right away that he and Carson's dad had certain similarities; for starters, they both liked quizzes. And Mr. Lipman liked props! Whenever there was a classroom guessing game of any sort, Mr. Lipman put on his woolen tweed detective's cap, with a brim in the front and a brim in the back. He strolled around like Sherlock Holmes, his hands clasped behind his back.

In Mr. Lipman's class, there were no rules.

Only life skills, like respect, responsibility, integrity,

compassion, loyalty, friendship, and the others. And guidelines, which were rules in disguise.

Mr. Lipman made sure the kids shared the responsibilities of the classroom, and he had deputies to help him. He also had Shape It Up to Shipshape for ten minutes every afternoon, so he wouldn't get stuck with cleaning up after a bunch of kids at the end of every day.

There were many, many guidelines. In fact, there were more guidelines than Carson could keep straight.

Guidelines for this, guidelines for that.

There were even guidelines for school celebrations, and they were posted on the wall: limit drinks with added sugar; limit overly sweet, too-sugary birthday treats.

The guidelines were reasonable enough; Carson liked making healthy food choices. At Montessori school, a nutritious lunch and snack were provided for the students every day, which often included fresh produce from the garden.

But at Montessori, birthday days were different. The birthday kid walked around carrying a globe while the parent told stories about the kid's life, like how old Carson was when he was adopted by his dad. When he first took the training wheels off his bicycle, and his first home run playing T-ball.

Then came the birthday cake, and all bets were off.

Every year, Carson's grandma baked Carson's all-time favorite: her famous You Gotta Be Kidding Me! Chocolate Calamity Cake. It was made of three layers of fudgy chocolate cake, with creamy chocolate icing between every layer and piled on top, and it had HAPPY BIRTHDAY, CARSON written across the top.

Everyone had a small piece.

Keyword: small.

Carson had no clue as to what he and his dad might do about a classroom birthday celebration at Valley Oak, but at least he had something to go on: there had already been one, Nancy's. Actually, it was Nancy's Faux Birthday celebration, with "faux" pronounced like "pho," rhyming with "toe," and basically meaning phony.

Nancy's For-Real Birthday was over the summer. In cases such as Nancy's, a Faux Birthday was celebrated in the classroom sometime before school was out.

For Nancy's Faux Birthday, her mom had provided

the Ultimate Not-Too-Gooey Faux-Birthday Birthday Treat. It even had a theme: endangered species, which they were studying in science.

First, Nancy's mom set up shop. She wiped off the counters with disinfecting wipes and fanned them dry.

Nancy had voiced one small request: that no one sing "Happy Faux Birthday," because she hated the "Happy Birthday" song.

Instead, she asked that everyone sing "Take Me Out to the Ball Game" and sing "Oakland A's" after the "root root root" part.

Weston Walker screamed "Giants!" instead.

Mr. Lipman wrote *Weston Walker* on the board.

Nancy's mom then asked everybody to wash their hands carefully and line up.

There were two endangered choices: endangered choice number one was a generous scoop of vanilla frozen yogurt in a white bowl with two red grapes for eyes, a big, round purple grape for a nose, and shredded coconut piled on either side of the grape for whiskers.

Endangered choice number two was a scoop of chocolate frozen yogurt with two purple grapes for eyes, a shiny, wrinkled pitted prune stuck in the middle for the nose, and some shredded coconut for whiskers.

Carson went for the vanilla polar bear. He liked chocolate sea otters but wasn't a prune fan.

Nancy's mom had also brought individual recyclable packets of 100 percent cranberry juice with straws attached in germ-free plastic sleeves.

Weston unwrapped the straw, threw the plastic on the floor, poked the straw into the packet, and spritzed Cody.

Mr. Lipman put a check by *Weston Walker* on the board.

"I always have a cake made out of turkey for my birthday," Wes announced.

He wiped his mouth with his sleeve. "I kid you not!"

"Use a napkin, Weston," Mr. Lipman told him.

Yikes, thought Carson.

A turkey cake?

That was going overboard on the not-overly-sweet-or-too-gooey guidelines.

"Put the napkin in the trash, Weston, not on my desk."

"I'm just setting it there for a minute! I may need to wipe my mouth again. Or blow my nose."

"Weston? Trash can. And if you want to apply for the Deputy Dustbuster position on the next jobs rotation, as you *say* you do, you're going to have to demonstrate that you have the life skills required to make appropriate use of a trash can and recycle box."

"Okay."

"You've got to be responsible, hardworking, and willing to put in the extra time and effort needed to do a good job."

"Fine, I will."

Wes crumpled up the napkin, jumped up for the long shot, and threw it into the corner. It sailed across the room. "Eeeeeeee-yeah!" he shouted when it landed in the trash.

"Sorry," he said.

Wes was pretty good at basketball.

That would have been a three-pointer.

3. HELLO,
Mr. Nibblenose

Dustbusting didn't require much talent, but it was a position of trust and responsibility. Chloe and Zoe were the current Co-deputy Dustbusters. And they were an extraordinary team, even taking extra time during Shape It Up to Shipshape to painstakingly dust things high up, low down, and way back—on the shelves and inside the cupboards.

Carson wouldn't have wanted the position.

He wasn't sure if he would want Nancy's position on the next rotation, or qualify for it, either: Nancy was Numbers Deputy—in charge of all number-related things, such as counting, dividing kids into equal teams, and helping Mr. Lipman correct math homework.

But Carson most definitely had his eye on Patrick's job: Deputy Pet Care Giver. That would be his goal. He wasn't sure if he would be ready to apply on the next jobs rotation, but maybe on a rotation after that.

Patrick knew a lot about caring for animals. His mom had founded the Wildlife Rescue Center. On Career Day, Patrick's mom brought in a Cooper's hawk named Coop. Coop had flown into a car windshield out by Green Gulch. After many weeks of rehabilitation, he had recovered from a broken wing and was almost ready to be released back into the wild.

Coop glared out from inside a pet carrier with his intense, beady orange eyes. He was zeroing in on something across the room.

Coop tipped his head, lifted his wings.

Then he screamed and everybody jumped.

Patrick's mom handed her blue Wildlife Rescue Center jacket to Patrick, and he covered Mr. Nibblenose's cage.

Mr. Nibblenose was a very reclusive, very wide, very well-fed, very glossy, somewhat socialized brown and white rat with a pink nose, soft pink ears, and a long, scaly gray tail.

He, too, was new—a gift to the class from a neighbor of Mr. Lipman's, a woman named Belinda who had moved to Belize.

Mr. Nibblenose was spending most of his time in his cage in an empty Fluff Puff tissue box with his tail sticking out of the hole. He was just getting used to the classroom, and the kids weren't allowed to handle him yet.

Except Patrick.

Carson wasn't sure how he felt about confining a rat to a cage for such a big part of every day. And he didn't know if Mr. Nibblenose would ever learn to enjoy the attention and company of the children.

He seemed quite shy.

When Coop spied him, Coop fluffed his feathers, flapped, opened his beak, poked his tongue out, and screeched.

Carson wasn't sure how Mr. Nibblenose felt about being cooped up in a cage, but he was 100 percent positive it freaked Mr. Nibblenose out to have a hawk scream at him.

Releasing Mr. Nibblenose into the wild, however, wouldn't be an option. He wasn't a wild rat—like a roof rat, jumping from roof to roof through the city with a group of rowdy rodent friends.

He wasn't a pack rat, either. And he wouldn't enjoy scuttling around in an automotive-repair garage, leering over the tops of empty cans, hoping to set up shop in an engine compartment.

He wasn't a sly dump rat like Templeton in *Charlotte's Web*, scavenging through garbage for stinky, rotten morsels of food, although Mr. Nibblenose certainly didn't look like he'd skipped many meals.

He was a meek splotchy-brown and bright-white domesticated pet rat with no experience in the wild. If released and allowed to go free, he would be quickly pounced upon by a cat or spotted from above by a predatory bird such as a Cooper's hawk. Being extremely hefty, Mr. Nibblenose would find it hard to scurry to safety.

When Carson was a veterinarian, he'd have to know how to evaluate and treat pet rats for various injuries and ailments, so he'd better get used to the idea of people having them for pets.

He would encourage his clients to create a Free-Range Roaming Rat Arena somewhere in their homes so rats could get out and about as much as possible.

Mr. Lipman must have noticed how interested Carson was in Mr. Nibblenose. And must also have guessed how much Carson wanted to make a new friend. So he suggested, "Why not be Patrick's Assistant Deputy Pet Care Giver?"

Patrick showed Carson how to make entries in the Nibblenose Classroom Care Notebook. They skimmed through the *Caring for Your Pet Rat* book together.

At recess, Carson helped Patrick clean the cage. And Patrick demonstrated how a rat can come when called. He called Mr. Nibblenose's name, and Mr. Nibblenose ran to his cage and squeezed back into his Fluff Puff hideout.

In the *Caring for Your Pet Rat* book, it showed examples of inexpensive and entertaining rat toys, such as the Birthday Prize in Disguise Surprise.

To make a Birthday Prize in Disguise Surprise, you had to individually wrap treats like yogurt drops, seeds, nuts, and other edibles inside small pieces of paper towel or newspaper. One by one, you then dropped them into a paper-towel roll until the roll was stuffed with individually wrapped treats. The next step was to fold both ends closed and hang it from the top of the cage.

Let the fun begin!

An alternative birthday treat was a sock piñata filled with goodies.

Carson didn't know when Mr. Nibblenose's birthday was, or if he would be interested in opening any presents.

Right now, all he seemed interested in doing was hiding in the Fluff Puff hut, mostly backward, but sometimes frontward, with his pale pink nose protruding from the hole and trembling in the air.

Carson figured he'd up his chances of becoming Deputy Pet Care Giver if he demonstrated to Mr. Lipman that he was responsible, and a hard worker, and willing to put in extra time and effort.

He'd start by earning some extra credit.

He thumbed through the Extra-Credit Bonus-Bucks Booklet on the counter near Mr. Lipman's desk, looking for something that would demonstrate his interest in animals.

> Word Find: Make a list of fifty-five
> five-letter words out of the letters in
> Valley Oak Elementary School. Recite
> the list.
> **TEN BONUS BUCKS**

> Oink! Bark! Honk! Make a list of at
> least seventy-five onomatopoeias, put
> them in alphabetical order, and sing
> the list for the class, set to the tune of
> "Twinkle, Twinkle, Little Star."
> **TEN BONUS BUCKS**

No thanks on that one.

> Whiz Quiz poem: Write a rhyming
> poem about an endangered species
> that showcases several examples
> of alliteration and onomatopoeia.
> Be accurate in regard to habitat and

physical description. Be prepared to
present it to the class.
TEN BONUS BUCKS

Carson wasn't good at talking in front of a class, but he wanted to get better at it. Bonus Bucks were an incentive.

Yay for Bonus Bucks!

When you earned a Bonus Buck, you could write your name on it and drop it into the slot in the top of the Bonus Bucks Box in the office.

Once a week there was a drawing; if your Bonus Buck was chosen, you got to spin the Bonus Bucks Wheel of Fortune and win a prize, such as a No-Homework Pass, which Carson would love to have.

The Wheel of Fortune was a handmade contraption, constructed of plywood and nails, banged together by the office manager, Mrs. Sweetow.

Last week Weston Walker had been awarded one Bonus Buck from Mr. Lipman for leaving Mr. Nibblenose completely alone.

And last week, with just one buck in the box, Wes was the Spinner Winner!

But something unfortunate happened to the Wheel of Fortune. Wes whirled the wheel so fast and hard the base toppled off the table and flopped onto the floor, and the wheel broke into several pieces.

Fortunately, the marker was intact. It pointed to a free Valley Oak sweatshirt.

Mrs. Sweetow reluctantly gave Wes his prize.

Wes told her that squirrels gave him the heebie-jeebies. But Mrs. Sweetow wouldn't trade for the acorn one because she was mad.

Carson wasn't sure if she'd repaired the wheel yet, or if it was even fixable, for that matter. But he decided on Whiz Quiz poem.

Hmmmmm. What animal would it be?

Carson stood there thinking.

"Carson?" said Mr. Lipman. "Math time."

Oops!

The rest of the kids had already lined up.

Three days a week, Carson switched classes for math. Carson, Patrick, Nancy, and some others trooped over to Ms. Parker's class, and some of Ms. Parker's kids went to Mr. Lipman's class.

Carson knew that there were yays and boos about

every situation, including being the New Kid at Valley Oak School.

And he had to say it: the biggest, fattest number-one boo was for Math Switcheroo. Ms. Parker herself was great.

One problem, though: she was overly neat.

In fact, a Neat Freak.

She had recently held a classroom event called Clean Out That Backpack, Dagnabbit! Day.

That wasn't a problem for Carson, first because he wasn't in her regular class, and second because his pack hadn't had the chance to accumulate debris.

However, because he had her for Switcheroo, he was subjected to a different Neat Freak issue: her Select Reject Button.

Ms. Parker's Select Reject Button was a cardboard picture of an apple with a bucktoothed worm poking its head out, and the apple was pushpinned to the wall just above the recycle bin.

If you turned in a math paper that was a rumpled or smudged mess, or if the problems were written with uneven columns, she'd just press the apple and say *Beeeep!*

Beeeep! meant place your paper in the bin below and begin again. Three *beeeep*s on the same assignment got you a blue slip: recess confined to a Blue Box.

The Blue Boxes were number two on the Boos List.

They were big, flat, bright blue squares painted on the asphalt on the playground.

And while Carson was on the topic of Boxes to Boo About: a big, fat, resounding boo on the June Box.

The June Box was a cardboard box decorated with colorful yarn that sat on the counter right next to Mr. Lipman's desk. Anybody who brought in candy or a toy and got caught with it had to put it into the June Box. At the moment, a fish was in there. It was a rubber bass screwed onto an oval wooden plaque with its mouth wide open and a fake fishing fly hanging off its lower lip.

There it would stay, cooped up till the end of the year, along with a fluorescent green light-up yo-yo, a package of peppermint pink Teenie-Weenie Jelly Beanies, and a trail of ants.

When Carson and his dad emailed the folks in Pasadena, Carson tried to report more yays than boos. He had to think awhile to come up with yays. But he wanted to think positively and make the best of his new situation.

So, yay for Bonus Bucks.

Yay for PE. He could have skipped the Hula-Hooping, but at least he was improving.

Yay for Career Day. He hoped a veterinarian would show up.

Yay for the Classroom Campout, which was just around the corner. Moose wouldn't be invited along on that one.

4. HELLO,
Hello Bingo

Carson heard the tinkly sound of Mr. Lipman's Chill-Time Chimes and looked up from his book.

"Class? I have completed a new Hello Bingo card, in honor of Carson. Sound good? Golf clap," he reminded the students.

They quietly clapped.

Wes whistled through his teeth.

Carson wished he could do that.

Mr. Lipman wrote *Weston Walker* on the board, and then slowly walked around the room, giving each student a sheet of paper with a bingo grid on it. Every box in the grid had an activity in it.

"Carson?" said Mr. Lipman. "So here's the dealio: Each person can sign their name in one box per card. Just one. You can also sign your own card. But just once.

"How the game works," continued Mr. Lipman, "is this: You try to fill the whole card with signatures. It's called Hello Bingo, and it's worth twenty Bonus Bucks.

"You all walk around and q-u-i-e-t-l-y interview other students, to get signatures on your card. So if Patrick, for example, rode a horse recently, he would sign *Patrick Tapp* in the 'Rode a horse' box."

"Did you, Patrick?" asked Shelly.

"Not me." Patrick shook his head. "No way."

"Why not?"

"Why not? Clues: summer camp, horse in a hurry, low branch, blackberry brambles, and beehive."

Whoa!

"No one on earth is getting me on horseback again."

Wes swaggered over to Carson.

"Gimme your card," he told Carson. "I rode horses all last summer. At my aunt Boo and uncle Hunk's quarter-horse farm in Cleveland."

He reached for Carson's card.

"Don't believe him," Cody warned. "He's a complete and total l-i-a-r."

Carson pulled it back. "No thanks, Wes. But thanks anyway."

"Well, I recently spoke a second language," said Wes. "I spoke Igpay Atinlay with my grandma. Fork over your card, buddy. I'll sign the 'Spoke a second language' box."

"Actually, I don't think Pig Latin would qualify," Carson told him.

But Wes grabbed Carson's card out of his hand. "Then how about the 'Took a class at the community center' box?"

Cody snatched it from Wes and handed it to Carson. He growled at Wes, "Get a clue, dude. He doesn't want you to sign in any of his boxes! And neither do I!"

Chloe and Zoe hurried over. "But we dooooo! You took a class at the community center?" said Chloe. "What kind of class?"

"Want to trade sweatshirts with me?" Wes asked Chloe.

"*Me* trade sweatshirts with *you*?" said Chloe. "Are

you size S? No, you're not." She began snapping her fingers. "Come on, come on. What kind of community class, Wes?"

"I asked for the acorn logo. But no, no. Mrs. Sweetow wouldn't give it to me. Even when I explained that squirrels give me the willies."

"Too bad. Next time don't smash up her wheel. And don't change the subject. What community class did you take?" Chloe asked.

Wes looked at the ceiling. "Well, what I took was . . . um."

Cody asked, "So exactly what kind of whopper is the King of Whopperland dishing up now?"

Zoe said, "Shhhh! Don't interrupt his train of thought. He's trying to remember a community class he took."

"You mean, trying to *make up* a community class he took?" Cody asked.

"It was a community sewing class!" said Wes. "It was a class called . . . um . . . Anyway, I sewed a denim tote bag. I did! With a cat on the front with one eye winking. With a rhinestone inside its eyeball."

Cody looked at Chloe and Zoe and raised his palms in the air. "How does he come up with this stuff?"

He walked away, muttering to himself.

Zoe asked Wes, "So, Wessie. How exactly do you get a rhinestone inside a cat eye on a piece of cloth?"

At first, Wes didn't answer. Then he said, "Well . . . there's little sharp prongs and you push 'em through the denim and put in the rhinestone and squash it down with a silver tool. But I didn't wait my turn for the tool. I pushed it by hand and poked my finger. I still have a scar."

"Let's see it," said Zoe.

"Yeah, show us da boo-boo," said Chloe.

Wes held his finger up. "It healed."

Chloe smiled a crooked little smile. "That was quick."

They gave their cards to Wes, and Wes signed them both in the "Took a class at the community center" box.

Zoe and Chloe high-fived each other and walked away, laughing.

Carson kept his distance from Wes.

He collected signatures for "Read a novel," "Played the piano," "Went bowling," and many others.

No one in the class said they had gone fishing, not even Weston.

Carson signed a lot of "Ate anchovy pizza" boxes. His was a sought-after signature because nobody liked little salty fish bits on their pizza, but Carson loved 'em!

He strolled around the room, stopping to peer into the June Box. "Don't tell anybody, but that there is actually my brother Joey's yo-yo," whispered Chloe. "I brought it to school, and Zoe gave it to Parks Johnson to play with during Math Switcheroo, and he got it taken away! Poor little yo-yo."

She looked sideways at Zoe.

"You told me to let Parks play with it," Zoe reminded her.

"I know, but you shouldn't have listened."

Chloe turned to Carson: "Joey keeps asking me if I've seen it!"

Zoe giggled into her hand. "The kid doesn't even know his yo-yo's trapped in the June Box."

"It's not funny," Chloe told her.

"Yes it is!" said Zoe. "Mr. Lipman is clueless! He thinks it's Parks's yo-yo! Parks is just going along with it, and pretending the yo-yo is his, because Chloe doesn't want Mr. Lipman to know she brought it to school and I don't want him to know I loaned it to Parks. And Parks couldn't care less whether Chloe's brother Joey's yo-yo is in the June Box till June!"

Zoe patted the top of Chloe's head. "Don't worry, Chloe, Joey will get it back . . . eventually. We'll see to that."

Wes wandered over. "That fish sings—press its head."

Zoe whispered, "Enter: Whopperman!"

Carson stepped back.

Wes said, "Press it! I'm serious, it sings!"

"By the way," Wes told Zoe. "I know more yo-yo tricks than Parks, in case you didn't know."

Zoe glanced at Mr. Lipman. He was standing with his back to them. "Let's see some!" she whispered.

"Yeah!" whispered Chloe.

Carson hurried away and sat down. Out of the corner of his eye, he saw some commotion by the June Box.

Mr. Lipman rang the chimes. "Time's up. So for now, it's ciao, farewell, good day, sayonara, adieu, adios, au revoir, auf Wiedersehen, and good-bye to Hello Bingo."

Then he held up his Quiet Coyote Hand—his middle two fingers against his thumb, and his pinkie and pointing finger sticking straight up, like coyote ears.

He rotated his hand, as if it was a coyote surveying the class. Then he wiggled the ears in Wes's direction because Wes was talking.

A few kids put up a Quiet Coyote Hand.

Not many, because that was a first-grader sign.

Wes put up two Quiet Coyote Hands, held them nose to nose, and made snarling noises. He attacked one hand with the other.

"Wes?"

Wes yipped and howled.

Then was quiet.

Mr. Lipman put a check by *Weston Walker* on the whiteboard and tapped on the schedule. *QUICK WRITE: Write a friendly thank-you letter to someone. Heading, date, greeting, body, closing, and signature.*

"We're focusing on the form. Don't forget those commas!"

A short time later, Mr. Lipman said, "Okay. Volunteers?"

Zach raised his hand. He read: "Dear Hat, Thank you for making me look like a hunk. From, Zach."

Mr. Lipman frowned. "Try again, Zachary. Show some appreciation for a person who has done something special for you. Also, you forgot the heading and the date."

Carson wrote the heading and the date and then:

Dear Dr. Tichenal,

Thank you for saving Genevieve's life when she was a puppy. We are all doing well up here in El Cerrito. We haven't met the new vet yet. But thanks for the referral.

I am just about nine now, and so of course I have outgrown stuffed animals. However, I appreciate how you handled the situation with Moose when I was a little kid. The stitches held up well. I still have your business card. You inspired me to go into veterinary medicine.

From,
Carson Blum

. . .

When Carson got home, he located the business card in his small treasure box and addressed the envelope to Dr. Tichenal.

He showed the letter to his dad. "Good letter, son."

"Thanks, Dad."

Carson, his dad, and Genevieve walked to the mailbox on the corner, and Carson dropped the letter into the slot.

Then he took a folded paper out of his back pocket. "This one's for you."

Carson's dad read it:

Dear Dad,

Thank you for everything you do for me. Thank you for arranging your schedule so you can drop me off and pick me up from school. I look forward to seeing you every afternoon. Let's celebrate your new job and our first two successful weeks in El Cerrito by going to Buster's Barbecue.

I love you, Dad.

From,
Carson

5. HELLO,
Buster's Barbecue

Buster's Barbecue may not have been the best place to do homework, but Carson brought it along anyway and worked on it on a picnic table covered with a checkered plastic tablecloth in the outdoor eating area.

Besides wanting to celebrate a new job and two weeks in El Cerrito together, Carson's dad wanted to check out his competition: he was pretty sure he was the best barbecuer in town, but you never know. He'd read a lot of great reviews about Buster's.

They both ordered the tri-tip dinner with two sides.

Carson's dad chewed thoughtfully. "Not bad . . .

maybe we should come here to Buster's after the birthday trail ride."

Carson whispered, "Nah! You got this guy beat, Dad. Let's you barbecue, at home after the trail ride! Here's to getting through the first two weeks!" Carson added cheerily.

They toasted each other with bottled water and iced tea.

Keeping smears and smudges of barbecue sauce off his homework was proving to be a bigger challenge than Carson expected. Plus, he got a huge splatter of sauce on his sleeve.

"No worries. I'll wash it and toss it into the dryer."

"Thanks, Dad."

Carson's dad showed him how to draw pictures to help with word problems. "And don't forget the labels, like minutes or pickles or whatever," his dad reminded him.

"Okay. There's potato salad on your ear, Dad."

Carson closed his math book.

Next. Language-arts homework. Paragraphs. Again. Choose a topic sentence from a list and write a paragraph. The list included "Soccer is a great game,"

"Hiking is a great sport," "A dog makes a great pet," and "Or choose your own topic sentence."

With the goal of becoming Deputy Pet Care Giver in mind, Carson wrote his topic sentence: *Rats are remarkable*.

Next he wrote:

Rats are playful. They really know how to have fun, and their toys are inexpensive. A toy can be as simple as a paper-towel roll, if the rat is able to squeeze in. Rats have life skills. They're brave and loyal. They're protective of their owners. A rat has been known to bite a robber's nose and chase it out of a house. Rats are intelligent. They can be taught tricks, like how to come when called. Rats are frisky. They like to exercise. They also like to hang out in roomy, clean cages, with fresh water and an assortment of fresh fruits and vegetables, not just rat blocks.

The next best thing to being an outdoor rat is being a very loved indoor rat with a Free-Range Roaming Rat Arena. Rats freak some people out, but others find them attractive animals.

Whew!

Done.

Carson's dad was looking over and reading Carson's paragraph as he wrote it.

"Protective? Well, that's quite a claim. . . . Bit a robber's nose? What evidence do you have to back that up?"

"A sworn statement from Weston Walker."

"Ah."

Carson's dad poked into his small plastic container of ranch beans. "So we'll take that with a grain of salt, as they say. . . ."

"I thought you didn't like ranch anything, Dad."

"Ranch beans are the rare exception to my ranch rule." He ate a few bites. One bean fell on his collar and rolled down into his shirt. "I'll shake it out later. So rats can come when called? Who told you that? Wes again?"

"Nope. I saw with my own eyes."

"You called him?"

"Patrick did."

"And he came running? Remarkable. Hmmm." He took a big gulp of iced tea and looked sideways at Carson.

"Well, he doesn't really run right *straight to you*, Dad, but he comes eventually. Anyway, on to alliteration!"

Carson wrote: *Raquelle the raucous raccoon really ran like a rocket.*

"Next I'll work on my extra-credit alliteration and onomatopoeia Whiz Quiz poem. I'm goin' for ten Bonus Bucks and a chance at the Bonus Bucks Wheel of Fortune! And maybe win a No-Homework Pass. Wahoo!"

"Eight years of university training and I have to be honest: I forget! What *is* onomatopoeia?"

"Don't ask me!"

Carson and his dad bused their own dishes. His dad quietly and politely burped into his fist near the recycling can and then tipped his Porsche cap good-bye to Buster. They headed to the car.

"There's a napkin stuck to your shoe, Dad."

"Right."

At home, Carson's dad looked up "onomatopoeia" in his big Webster's dictionary. "Oh, it's a word like 'buzz.' Or 'click.' Or 'zoom.' Like: When I clicked my camera at a buzzing bumblebee, it zoomed after me. And I plopped in the muck."

Carson smiled. "I'm glad you didn't get hurt, Dad.

Does a blob of goopy chocolate yogurt plopped into a waffle cone at the International Yogurt Depot sound good to you?"

"I have no idea how one small yogurt shop on the corner claims to be an 'international' yogurt depot, but let's go."

When they arrived back home, Genevieve was lying with her nose between her paws and a scrap of torn paper stuck to her nostrils with $21,783 + 72,634$ written on it. She thumped her tail. She rolled her eyes to the side.

"It was my fault, Dad," Carson quietly said. "It had barbecue sauce on it. Can one page of math problems hurt her?"

"Nah."

"Just making sure."

"Remember the antler incident, Dad?"

"How could I forget that."

Bedtime, nine o'clock, was quickly approaching. Carson started his math homework all over again.

He thought of Ms. Parker and called out: "Is 'beeping' an onomatopoeia?"

"Yes."

"Is 'buzzing'?"

"Yes."

Carson painstakingly redid his math problems and then worked for a few minutes on his Whiz Quiz poem.

In the morning, he made his bed and sat Moose on top of the dresser, next to the cockeyed pencil jar Carson's dad had made in a college ceramics class. Moose enjoyed sitting there and looking across the room at the wallpaper.

It was a pretty morning, with sunshine coming through the blinds and making a pattern of bright yellow lines on the wall.

"Want to try to guess the animal in my Whiz Quiz poem?" Carson asked his dad during breakfast. "I'm trying to make it really tricky. I really want to trick my class. And Mr. Lipman! Ready?"

"Shoot."

"Face round as a balloon."

"Panda."

"No."

"Skunk?"

"A skunk has a pointy face, Dad."

"Not all do. Remember when you were a skunk for Halloween? Grandma made that costume. You were a short skunk with a round face and a big, fat, fluffy black and white tail."

"Being away from Grandma and Grandpa stinks," Carson said.

"Boy, you can say that again."

"Being away from Grandma and Grandpa stinks," Carson said.

And sometimes Valley Oak stank.

6. HELLO,
Mrs. Crabbly

For the past two weeks, Carson hadn't known if he was coming or going.

He heard the Chill-Time Chimes and looked up.

Okay.

Was he coming or going?

He glanced again at the schedule written on the board, just to make sure: Going.

This time to the computer lab.

After that, lunch.

Carson took his lunch from his Valley Oak backpack hanging on his hook—right next to Chloe's, near the rolling book cart by the classroom door.

He stood in line, carefully holding the brown paper bag with *Carson* written on the front. He was starving! Inside was a tri-tip sandwich on whole wheat bread with lettuce and tomato, three home-baked oatmeal cookies, a small handful of all-fruit gummy bears that were *not* candy, and a foil container of guava juice *without* added sugar.

All the other kids had canvas lunch bags. Shelly's sparkled: on the side it had a unicorn with twinkly wings and a twisted white twinkly horn flying over a rainbow.

Carson was fine with his regular old plain brown paper lunch bag, but there was quite a bit of lunch in it today. He would carry it carefully and remember to bring home the small plastic packet of Eskimo Ice so his dad could freeze it again.

Carson surveyed the line of lunches. Nancy's MON-TEREY BAY AQUARIUM bag was the best. It had a brown baby sea otter lying on its back in the white foam, holding a clam on its belly and looking right at you.

"Where's the Monterey Bay Aquarium?" Carson asked her.

"In Monterey by the bay."

Nancy cracked a smile.

"I have a sea otter named Ethel that looks just like this." She held the bag up so Carson could get a really good look. "Or she did when she was young, anyway. Ethel's a bit ratty-looking at the moment, but she was once a very sleek lady. You'll meet her on Stuffed Animal Day. She's getting all dressed up and wearing lipstick. Are you bringing a stuffed animal on Stuffed Animal Day, Carson?"

"Nope."

"Why not?"

Carson kept quiet.

"Last month that kid named Parks in Ms. Parker's class brought in a badger wearing green goggles and a mini Burton snowboarding beanie."

"He did?"

A Burton beanie was fine for a badger. A little lipstick was okay for an otter. But Moose kept it real: he just wore his own fur. Au naturel! His birthday suit was bedraggled due to severe snuggling when Carson was a toddler, but it was not ratty by any stretch of the imagination.

Or not *that* ratty by any stretch of the imagination.

Mr. Lipman stood in the doorway and waved to Mrs. Crabbly as she approached. "Hello, Abby! How was the seminar?"

"Good. Free pamphlet on PowerPoint pointers, free PowerPoint tote, free gold PowerPoint pen. Which I immediately lost. Unfortunately."

Mrs. Crabbly was wearing a plastic battery-operated cuckoo-clock pin, and Carson wondered if a bird popped out of the hole in it.

"How was my substitute?"

"Lousy!" moaned Sydney. "She made us label pictures of laptops in the library and didn't let us go into the lab! And it was bor-ring."

"Any-way! We have a new student," Mr. Lipman announced. "Carson Blum."

"Welcome to the New Kid!" Wes sang out. He slung his arm around Carson and tripped on him. Both boys toppled over.

"Wes? Please. Take it easy!" Mr. Lipman helped them to their feet. "You okay, boys?"

Carson picked his lunch bag up and inspected it.

"Carson? This is the famous Mrs. Crabbly, computer teacher extraordinaire!"

"Wonderful to have you at Valley Oak, Carson!" Mrs. Crabbly said.

They shook hands.

"Be baby ducks!" called Mrs. Crabbly cheerily. "I'm the mama duck. Straight line please! And no quacking!"

Carson hugged his lunch against his chest. The kids followed Mrs. Crabbly across the playground, steering clear of Wes, who was swinging his canvas gorilla lunch bag around and quacking.

The computer lab was in the library, and no food or drinks were allowed inside. The class stopped at the back entrance to the lab to line their lunches up along the outside wall on a ledge protected by the overhang of the roof.

Wes got a little dizzy and off balance, and clobbered Carson on the back.

"Wes?" said Mrs. Crabbly. "You gotta be kidding me. Put that bag down, this minute. Are you okay, Carson?"

"He's fine," said Wes. "Put your lunch here next to mine, Cars. Between King Kong and the muskrat."

Nancy raised an eyebrow at him. "It's a sea otter, Weston. And you know it."

Mrs. Crabbly invited them into the lab. "I'm going to begin with a short PowerPoint demo. Nancy? You're Carson's helper."

Nancy sat down and tapped the chair beside her. Wes sat down on Carson's other side. "I'm also your helper," he told Carson. "Ask me anything."

Chloe and Zoe stood quietly in the doorway.

"Girls? How can I help you?"

Zoe pointed to Chloe. "You ask."

"No. You."

"You."

"You!"

"You."

"You!"

"Girls! Please! I've got nineteen kids waiting for me. What can I do for you?"

"Okay. May we please be PowerPoint partners, Mrs. Crabbly?" Zoe asked politely.

"Again?"

The girls nodded.

Mrs. Crabbly sighed. "One of these days I'd like to see some independent work out of you gals. You two stick together like glue!"

"Can we?" said Chloe. She poked her bottom lip out at Mrs. Crabbly. "Please?"

Mrs. Crabbly threw up her hands, and the girls scurried over to the computer on the other side of Nancy's and hopped onto the chair.

Mrs. Crabbly went to the demonstration computer. With her back to the class, she sat up straight in her chair, yanked on the hem of her skirt, placed her two feet on the floor, round toes of her shoes pointing straight ahead, and put both hands lightly on the keyboard. "Oops! Minor detail." She stood up again.

A little bird popped its head out of her cuckoo-clock pin and squeaked eleven times in a tiny voice. More like a beep than a squeak or peep. Carson couldn't see if its beak opened and its wings flapped or not.

"Machines work best when you turn them on," Mrs. Crabbly told the class. She pushed the button on the DVD player and the TV above it, then sat back down.

There was a rattling sound.

"Is that you, Wes?" Mrs. Crabbly said without looking away from her screen. "Leave the seat adjuster alone."

"Okay, everyone, so today we'll continue on with your PowerPoint slide show that showcases you, you, the wonderful you!

"We'll all add a favorite-foods slide. If you want to creep, crawl, fall, bounce, fly, or roll the letters in, just click on whatever it is that you want to animate and . . ."

She demonstrated.

"Anyone have a question?"

Wes began rolling his chair up to Mrs. Crabbly. "I do."

"That chair is not a vehicle. Stop!"

Wes made loud brake noises and screeched to a stop. "Can I go to the boys' room?"

"The pass is on my desk. No fooling around! I mean it!"

Mrs. Crabbly started to slowly proceed down the row of computers.

"I hate PowerPoint!" Sydney grumbled as Mrs. Crabbly approached her screen. "I hatehatehatehate-hate it."

Wes picked up the laminated hall pass strung on yarn and put it around his neck. He spied

Mrs. Crabbly's missing gold pen, which had rolled under her chair.

Wes picked up the pen and held it like a sword as he jumped through the doorway and out onto the asphalt.

Carson could hear him outside, making his awesome imitation of a semi blasting its horn.

Mrs. Crabbly closed her eyes, shook her head, and sighed deeply.

"However, Mr. Noiseman out there does remind me that if you want to, you can explore adding sound effects to your presentation. Listen up." She selected "frog croak" from the list of sounds on Sydney's computer.

"I hate frogs," grumbled Sydney.

"It's just an example!"

"I hate examples of frogs croaking even more than I hate frogs!"

7. HELLO,
Homesick

With Nancy's help, Carson logged on, launched PowerPoint, and typed *Carson Blum* in the title box and *That's Me* in the subtitle box.

"Watch," she told him. Nancy dragged a mini spring roll onto a slide and typed *Dim Sum—Yum!* above it. Then she clicked on the words and bounced them in, to the loud sound of a drumroll.

"Go," said Nancy.

She supervised as Carson typed *barbecue* in the search box. Carson chose a guy in a chef's hat standing near a grill holding a barbecue fork.

"Nice," said Nancy. "Now drag it on over."

Carson dragged it over and typed *Barbecue + My Dad = Rad!*

He flipped the words in, to applause: the loud sound of a crowd clapping.

Mrs. Crabbly glanced over at Carson's screen. "Your dad is a good barbecuer? What's his specialty?"

"Tri-tip."

Carson heard rapid Fourth of July rocket and explosion sounds outside the building. Wes stumbled in, panting. "I had to defend myself out there!"

Mrs. Crabbly said, "Sit. Down. Be. Quiet. Weston. I've had enough of this."

"I did! I had to launch a missile to fend off an air attack!"

Mrs. Crabbly heaved another sigh.

"I barely made it to the boys' room and back alive! I crawled here on my elbows! Look how dirty my pants are."

"Weston?" said Mrs. Crabbly. "Last warning."

She continued down the row of computers.

"How do you spell 'prosciutto'?" Eva asked her.

Weston sat down and looked over at Carson's

screen. "Your dad has a Porsche, doesn't he? I saw that old Porsche."

Carson stayed quiet.

"Do you know my grandma is a demolition-derby driver?" Wes asked.

"Here we go again," mumbled Cody.

"She drives a '74 Buick LeSabre demolition-derby car," continued Wes. "Which is better than a Porsche because it doesn't matter if you smash it up. You're supposed to!"

"Suresuresuresure," Cody said under his breath.

"Go back and do a slide on family," Nancy instructed Carson. "Then pets. And you'll be caught up!"

Carson searched for a dad carrying a briefcase and a house with flowers in the garden. He typed *Grandma* and found a woman fishing from a folding chair, and *Grandpa* and found a man fishing from a folding chair.

Chloe leaned in front of Nancy's computer screen and got really, really close to Carson and said behind her hand, "Have you ever heard the whopper Wes tells about his great-grandpa Daniel?"

"There's an ant on the end of your pinkie," Nancy

told her. "And if I were you, I'd get busy. Mrs. Crabbly is watching."

Chloe softly blew the ant off at Carson and giggled.

Her breath smelled like peppermint, like mint chip ice cream, like he always got when he went out for ice cream with his grandma and grandpa. And when Carson caught the scent of that hint of mint, a wave of being homesick washed over him.

He looked at the screen, and the images got blurry; there were tears in his eyes. He blinked them away.

A birthday without Grandma and Grandpa?

What would that be like?

Carson was grateful that Nancy wasn't watching him. She had turned her focus to Wes, trying to help him focus.

"We're on favorite foods now, Wes. So get with the program, okay? Mrs. Crabbly is getting really irked at you, mister. No more noises! Use the sound effects on the computer. And why don't you put on your headphones. Just a thought."

Wes put on his headphones.

"They work best when you plug them in!" Nancy

added. She plugged them in for Wes. "Remember. Favorite food!"

"Huh?"

Wes took off his headphones.

"Huh?"

"Favorite food!" Nancy told him.

Wes clicked on the little speaker at the bottom of the screen and cranked up the volume.

There was a loud explosion and Wes tumbled off his chair. "Whoa!!!" he yelled.

Suddenly Mrs. Crabbly said, "Wes? You're outta here."

Wes stood up. "But my chili cheese dog blew up!"

Mrs. Crabbly stormed to her desk and jerked open the drawer. "Where's my pen?" she muttered. "Never mind . . ." She took out a pencil and scribbled a note. "Take this to the principal's office. I've had it."

Mrs. Crabbly shook the note at Wes. "Take it."

He stared at the ground.

She pointed to the door. "Out! And pick up your lunch when you go. Eat on the bench outside of the office."

"But—"

"Outoutout!" cried Mrs. Crabbly.

"But . . ."

She began to count. "Ten . . . nine . . . eight—"

"But . . ."

"Seven . . ."

"But . . ."

"Six . . ."

"But . . ."

"Don't but, but, but, but, but me, Mr. Walker! Out you go!"

Wes pointed at her large black clog. "But you're standing on my shoelace!"

Mrs. Crabbly frowned. "Sorry. I'll suspend the count while you tie it."

"Will you start at ten again?"

"No. We're at five. And double-knot that bow."

Wes tied his shoelace and stood up.

"Ready?" asked Mrs. Crabbly.

"Yup."

Starting the countdown: "Five . . ."

Wes s-l-o-w-l-y sauntered to the doorway, and paused on the threshold.

"Four . . ."

He casually rested his hands on both sides of the doorjamb and leaned out.

"Three . . ."

He gazed at the landscape.

"Twooooooooooooooo . . ."

Mrs. Crabbly marched to the phone and punched in the office number. She covered the receiver with her hand.

"One!"

Wes sprang out, twirled in the air, and landed on the asphalt. He glanced skyward, made a few karate chops in the air, and then disappeared from view.

Mrs. Crabbly crabbily spoke to the office manager: "I've had it. I've absolutely positively completely and totally had it with—

"Yes. You guessed it.

"Yes, I'm fine."

She hung up. "Brother!" She straightened her suit jacket and tucked her hair behind her ear.

"Mrs. Crabbly?" said Eva quietly. "I know what might make you feel a little better."

"What?"

"Take your glasses off the top of your head. They're pinching you and creating stress. And . . ."

"And what?"

"And maybe comb your hair a little bit. And touch up your lipstick. Just a suggestion!"

"Eva? This is not a salon. Get to business! I mean it!"

Mrs. Crabbly meant business. Everyone worked quietly.

Carson heard twelve tiny beeps. He snuck a peek to see if the beak opened.

It did!

The lunch bell rang.

Tri-tip time!

8. GOOD-BYE,
Tri-Tip Sandwich

Outside, the clouds were dark, but there were patches of blue. The gusty wind was damp; it blew Carson's collar up. He looked for his lunch.

Huh?

It was gone.

There was a small blue plastic packet of Eskimo Ice sitting near Nancy's MONTEREY BAY AQUARIUM bag, and that was it.

Carson looked around. There on the ground was what was left of—what?

His sandwich?

A circle of kids had gathered around.

His empty paper bag was floating across the ground,

carried away by the wind. The foil drink was speared. Guava juice had leaked onto the ground. There was nothing left in the plastic sandwich bag. One thin piece of tri-tip was hanging in a bush, a slice of bread in the dirt below it.

Crumbled oatmeal cookies were scattered.

All of his colorful sugar-free all-natural organic gummy bears made with real juice extract were thrown across the asphalt.

They sparkled in the sunshine like a rainbow of rubber jewels.

Don't cry, he told himself.

"I'll get Mrs. Crabbly," said Nancy quietly.

Soon Mrs. Crabbly hurried out. She stared at the mess. "Unbelievable. The principal and I will deal with the individual responsible for this. Any witnesses?"

The children said nothing.

Many left for the cafeteria. Others wandered off, lunches in hand.

Mrs. Crabbly sighed. "What. Next."

Nancy, Eva, Luciana, Oswaldo, and Patrick waited with Carson. Chloe and Zoe stood a few feet away.

"I'll share my lunch with you," Eva told Carson. "Do you like cold linguine with pesto?"

"Yes."

"Do you like ham and cheese on rye?" asked Patrick.

"Yes."

"Do you like leftover lasagna?" asked Shelly.

"Yes."

"Do you like freeze-dried, fried, pickled persimmon pudding?" asked Nancy. "With chocolate duck-billed platypus noses on top? Only kidding."

"Thanks, kids," Mrs. Crabbly told everyone. "But I'll arrange for a lunch for Carson in the cafeteria."

Mrs. Crabbly walked over and picked up her gold pen.

She clicked it a few times.

"Hmmmm," she muttered, "brand-new free pen I get from a seminar mysteriously goes missing from my desk. Discovered outside in the dirt with point broken. Lunch bag impaled and contents scattered. Put two and two together and what do you get?"

"Weston Walker," said Chloe and Zoe.

They walked away.

Patrick patted Carson on the back. "Don't feel bad. It's just Wes being Wes. Don't take it personally."

Oswaldo added, "Wes gets to fooling around and doesn't know when to quit."

"Sure you don't want half a ham sandwich?" Patrick asked.

"Nah, it's all right."

"Okay. See you on the field," Oswaldo told Carson. "Hang in there." He offered his fist for Carson to bump.

Mrs. Crabbly stepped back into the lab to call the office.

"It'll be okay," Nancy reassured Carson. "I think it's pizza day, and pizza's not bad here. I'd give it . . . mmmmm. Maybe a C-plus."

She smiled a little at Carson, which cheered him up.

Mrs. Crabbly came out carrying a wastebasket. On her way down the step, she slipped off the edge of one clog and almost fell over. "Mrs. Crabbly?" said Eva. "Those clogs are unsafe. For you, and those around you. You trampled on Wes's shoelace and could have tripped him. Plus, they look like gigantic licorice jelly beans."

She paused.

"And . . . did I hear you say a bad word?"

"Absolutely not. 'Dagnabbit' is not a bad word, and besides, I almost broke my ankle. Now run along, Eva. I've had enough style tips for one day."

"Fine, but I think you'd be safer wearing flats and not jelly beans."

"I heard you."

"Or maybe some heels—not too high. Really, they'd look better—with that skirt. And maybe lose the cuckoo accent pin."

Mrs. Crabbly made her eyes big at Eva. "Okay, okay—I get it!" she told her. "One trip to Italy and I've suddenly got a self-appointed fashion cop on my hands."

"I've been to Italy twice. Once with family and once with my aunt Liz."

"Fine. Ciao! It's lunchtime."

"We also went to Paris."

"Fine. Au revoir. That's French for scram."

She stooped down and picked up the empty sandwich bag and most of the gummy bears. "Just how I wanted to spend my lunch hour," she mumbled to herself. "Conducting an investigation of sandwich vandalization."

"Come on, Carson," said Nancy. She dragged Carson away by his sleeve. Luciana caught up to them and grabbed the other sleeve, and they towed him toward the cafeteria.

Carson sat with a bunch of other kids on a long table in the noisy cafeteria and ate cheese pizza and apple slices. He drank his carton of milk and ate three small fig bars. It wasn't barbecued tri-tip, but it was good!

But after lunch, he didn't feel like playing on the field.

He went outside and sat on a bench under the tall pine tree, alone. He missed Gavin and Case. What were they doing right now?

He missed Rainbow Ridge Montessori and everything about it.

He didn't understand why Wes would want to trash his lunch. What had he done to Wes?

Carson blinked back tears. He scooted over and moved into a patch of sunshine. It disappeared. Clouds were building on the horizon, and they looked like big gray bags of rain.

Pretty soon he saw Ms. Pierson heading his way

with Wes in tow. "Carson?" she called. "Wes has a note for you."

"Don't look at me," Wes called to Carson. "'Cause I didn't do it." He looked over at Ms. Pierson. "I didn't pierce anybody's lunch. And there are no witnesses and no proof!"

Ms. Pierson folded her arms on her chest and shook her head. "Whatever you say, Wes. Just give him the note."

Carson unfolded it. *Hey, New Kid* had been written and erased and changed to *Hey, Carson.* Then *I've just been told that somebody trashed your lunch but it wasn't me, it wasn't. From, Weston.*

Carson handed the note back to Wes.

"It was the sixth graders that did it," Wes said. "Bet you anything. Because just before I went up to the office, just as I was leaving the lab, out of the corner of my eye, I saw two sixth-grade girls stop in the yard and stare. This is how they looked. Like this."

Wes cupped his hand over his eyes, curled his upper lip back, bit his bottom lip with his front teeth, and wrinkled his nose like a rabbit.

It was so silly that if the situation hadn't been so serious, Carson would have laughed.

Ms. Pierson said, "I'm a busy woman, Wes. Too busy for nonsense. Back to the office you go!"

"Wait!" said Wes. He walked closer to Carson and unzipped his lunch bag. "Want half?"

"What is it?"

"A jam sandwich." Wes glanced at Ms. Pierson and whispered behind his hand, "And orange soda! Want a swig?"

"I already ate pizza and drank milk," said Carson. He paused.

"What kind of jam is it?"

"Strawberry. Actually, it's strawberry ice cream topping. Same difference."

"Are we allowed to have orange soda in our lunches at this school?" Carson quietly asked.

"Not *bottles* or *cans* of orange soda," Wes whispered. "But my orange soda is in an aluminum water container. And it's a small amount. A limited amount. And it's flat! No bubbles anymore, so it's not really soda. Do you want to come to my whole birthday party on Saturday the twenty-second at the demolition derby? My grandma is giving it for me. She has a pit pass."

A pit pass?

Wow!

So he wasn't telling a whopper about his grandma after all!

At this point, there was no actual proof that Wes had trashed Carson's lunch. It could have been someone else. It could have been sixth-grade girls. They were definitely persons of interest, under this particular set of circumstances. Since a birthday party at a car race was involved, Carson decided to give Wes the benefit of the doubt. He said, "I'll ask my dad."

"Tell him: six o'clock, twenty-second, Atlas Speedway. Bring the Porsche."

"Wes!" yelled Ms. Pierson. "Move it!"

Wes dug into his lunch bag, found his sandwich at the bottom, unwrapped the plastic wrap, pulled the sandwich in half, and gave half to Carson. Wes squeezed his half into a ball and stuffed it into his mouth. "Don't forget," he said with his mouth full. "The twenty-second!"

"Hop to it!" called Ms. Pierson.

Wes turned and stuck his tongue out in her direction.

"Knock it off," she called.

"I'm catching raindrops."

"It's not even raining!"

"Yes it is! See all the black spots on the asphalt?"

Carson sat back down and watched Wes and Ms. Pierson walk back to the office.

He ate his half of the jam sandwich.

Squishy white bread.

Mmm-mm!

A crow swooped down from the branches above and landed on the ground on one scaly, spindly leg. It flapped its wings at Carson and opened its black beak and squawked again. Then it flew onto the roof.

Looking up at the gutter, Carson saw the head of the crow, then the tail of the crow, then the head of the crow, then the tail of the crow.

He got up and wandered away.

Carson strolled around the yard.

The lunch bell rang. Carson and the kids filed into the classroom and sat down.

"Where's Wes?" asked Mr. Lipman.

"In the office."

"Again? What this time?"

"Well . . . let's just say there was an issue," said Chloe. "Involving Carson's lunch."

"And Mrs. Crabbly's lost gold pen," Zoe added. "Put two and two together and . . ."

Mr. Lipman put his hands on his hips and frowned. "Good gravy. Are you serious?"

Chloe and Zoe both closed their eyes and slowly nodded their heads.

"Carson got pizza, though," said Luciana. "We escorted him to the cafeteria."

"How was the pizza, Carson?"

"Good."

9. HELLO,
Bob

Carson was happy when school was over and his dad pulled up.

Genevieve was in the front seat! She slobbered a few kisses on Carson's neck and ear as he climbed into the back, and then she looked through the windshield and softly woofed at a crow flapping in a treetop.

"How did it go today?" Carson's dad asked as Carson buckled up.

"Great!"

Carson's dad began slowly driving out of the parking lot. "How was your lunch?"

"Fine! I had a double lunch. My original lunch got trashed."

"Your lunch got trashed? By who!"

"Not sure. Two sixth-grade girls are persons of interest. They were seen in the area looking suspicious. Like this. Look in the rearview mirror."

Carson shaded his eyes, scrunched up his nose, and bit his bottom lip.

"It took me twenty minutes to make that lunch!"

"Well, I got free pizza from some friendly ladies with nets on their heads in the cafeteria, and also Wes shared his sandwich with me."

"That was nice of him."

"And guess what. He invited us to his birthday party!"

"Really? A party invitation for the new kid on the block? Terrific!"

"It's a demolition-derby party. The whole thing is at Atlas Speedway. Six o'clock on the twenty-second."

His dad put on the brakes. "That's this Saturday! Let me get this straight: for this kid Wes's birthday party, his parents think I'm going to drag you out to a dilapidated old speedway?"

"His grandma does."

"His grandma is hosting this event? And this

86

woman thinks we're going to sit on rickety old bleachers? And watch a bunch of wrecked-up cars roar around a track in the mud? With their tires flat and their radiators belching steam? It's supposed to rain this weekend!"

"Can we, Dad?" said Carson.

"Are you kidding me?" He looked at Carson in the rearview mirror. "Of course!"

In the morning, Carson woke up, got dressed, ate breakfast, brushed his teeth, packed his pack, and played with Genevieve.

Carson loved playing with Genevieve but was hoping for some two-legged friends in the near future.

He was making some headway in the friendship department at school.

It was slow going, but he was beginning to feel more a part of things. Patrick and Oswaldo invited him into their games, and that helped.

And Nancy was always friendly.

He could depend on Nancy to be nice.

Luciana, Shelly, Sydney, Matthew, Zach, and the others were welcoming.

They waved hi and bye.

Maybe someone would invite him over to their house someday after school or on a weekend.

If it was Wes, Carson would say he was busy.

The next morning, right after the bell rang, Mrs. Crabbly appeared in the doorway of the class. She looked over the top of her glasses at the class and then at Mr. Lipman. "I'm sorry for the interruption."

A mouse head came out of her Swiss cheese pin and squeaked eight times.

"But I have an announcement." She turned to Wes. "First, I apologize to you, Weston, on behalf of myself and Ms. Pierson."

She turned back to the class.

"Thanks to the keen observations of two sixth-grade girls, we have now concluded that Carson's lunch was not, in fact, ripped to shreds by an individual wielding a gold pen."

She paused.

"The lunch was annihilated by a large black crow with a bent beak. A Nuisance Bird has been identified. We believe it is the same shabby individual who wintered here several years ago and went by the name of Bob. The sixth graders recognized Bob from when they were in kindergarten.

"A warning to all: if you get swooped down upon from above, do not launch objects into the air to defend yourself."

She turned to Wes: "And next time you find my pen under a chair, mister, give it back to me! Finders Keepers does *not* apply at this school, as you well know. And may I add that you also well know that a pen is not a projectile. A pen should not be thrown under any circumstances. Plus, you broke it."

She looked at Wes like she was boring a hole through his head with her eyeballs. "I didn't even get to use it once."

Then she said to the class, "If dive-bombed by a big belligerent bird with a slightly bashed-up beak, cover your head with your arm or hoodie hood and run away quickly. Then report the incident to the office. Carson?"

"Yes?"

"Ask your parent to buy you a Bob-proof lunch bag."

"Go to Shop Rite," said Eva. "It's out by the fairgrounds."

"And Atlas," added Wes.

Mrs. Crabbly looked over at Mr. Lipman. "I'm thinking of stopping by the Spring Campout for the evening barbecue and bringing my husband, Lee. If that's all right with you."

"By all means," said Mr. Lipman.

Carson couldn't wait to tell his dad what happened with Bob.

"Animal quiz, Dad," he said as he climbed into the car.

"Did they find out who trashed your lunch?"

"First clue: Claws. Carnivore."

"Tiger?"

"Black. Attacks from above."

"Panther?"

"Nope."

"Bear?"

"Bears don't attack from above, Dad. Next clue: Eats bears."

"Eats *bears*?"

"Small juicy ones."

"No way!"

"It does! It eats very small, very colorful juicy bears and large oatmeal cookies. . . . And tri-tip."

"What?!?!"

"Yup. A bird named Bob got my lunch, Dad."

"Weird. And he drank the guava juice?"

"Some of it."

"So it wasn't the girls or Wes who did it. That's good to know."

"I agree, but we need to get me a Nuisance Bird–proof canvas lunch bag, on the double."

"You can say that again!"

"But we need to get me a Nuisance Bird–proof canvas lunch bag, on the double."

They planned it perfectly. They would get the canvas bag, buy Wes a present, and pull into the entrance of Atlas Speedway at six o'clock sharp.

Late Saturday afternoon, Carson and his dad went to Shop Rite and selected a canvas lunch bag with a picture on it of two moose standing at the edge of a river with the Grand Teton mountain range in the background.

They bought a present for Wes and stuck it in a birthday bag with a tag on it. Carson borrowed

a pen from the cashier and signed it: *Your friend,*
Carson.

Carson heard a voice squeal: "Carson! Hey!"

It was Eva, and she hurried over, followed by a styl-
ish woman in a red dress and backless red high-heel
shoes. She was even wearing a red felt hat with a red
feather and a small black veil with a brim that sloped
down a little over one eye!

And matching red lipstick, and lots of it.

"This is my aunt Liz."

Everybody said hi.

"So I see you got a lunch bag," Eva said. "Awesome. Did you see the shorts on sale?"

Eva waved them over to a rack of shorts, 75 percent
off. "These would look *so* good on you, Carson." She
held up a big, baggy pair of navy blue shorts with a lot
of pockets and zippers.

Aunt Liz stood back and put her finger on her
cheek. "They look like they'd fit," she said. She
glanced at Carson's dad.

Carson's dad said, "Up to him!"

Aunt Liz walked a few feet away and waved a neon
green T-shirt on a hanger at Carson's dad. "Can you
believe it?" She checked the tag. "Two bucks."

She shook it at him. "Size L?"

"Sounds about right."

They all walked outside together and waved good-bye in the parking lot. Eva and her aunt zoomed off in a little red convertible.

"To be honest, I don't really know if I like baggy shorts with pockets and zippers all over them," Carson said as they got into the car.

"No worries. I'm sure we can return them if they don't work out." Then Carson's dad added, "Keep in mind that you don't have to change your style in order to fit in. And you don't have to fit in, regardless. Be yourself, son."

"I will, Dad. Do you like your new T-shirt?"

"Not that much, but it's the price of a greeting card."

"I've never seen you wear a Day-Glo T-shirt with a Nor Cal logo on it before, Dad."

"Well, we've never lived in Northern California before. And I'd also like to learn to snowboard sometime, since the mountains are closer now."

"You would? Me too!"

"Maybe we can take a trip to the snow before it melts."

"That's a great idea, Dad!"

Wow.

A trip to the snow—now that would be news-worthy!

So would the demolition derby! "Don't forget to take lots of pictures, okay, Dad? So we can email them to Case and Gavin!"

"I won't."

"Did I ever tell you that Abby Crabbly's husband's name is Lee? Lee and Abby Crabbly—see if you can say that five times fast without messing up!"

The brief T-shirt-and-shorts shopping expedition had thrown them off schedule, but not by much.

Before Carson's dad could properly say Lee and Abby Crabbly, Lee and Abby Crabbly, Lee and Abby Crabbly, Lee and Abby Crabbly, Lee and Abby Crabbly, they had pulled into Atlas Speedway.

Minor detail: Wes and his grandma weren't there. In fact, no one was there but them. There was no demolition derby at all—none. Nothing was going on. Just a chain-link fence, rickety bleachers, an empty racetrack, and a shut-down concession stand that had PIZZA HOT DOGS BURGERS FRIES ICE CREAM painted on the side. A sign that had fallen onto the ground said CLOSED UNTIL JUNE.

They went home.

Both had gotten into the mood for demolition-derby concession-stand food, so they picked up a package of hot dogs, a package of squishy buns, and a can of chili.

Carson's dad said, "There must have been some mistake about the date of the birthday party."

But there wasn't a mistake.

Wes told a whopper and Carson fell for it—hook, line, and sinker.

He felt bad about that.

Mad, too!

It was mean of Wes.

After dinner, he ripped the *Your friend, Carson* tag off the birthday bag. And threw it away.

"I hate Wes," Carson told his dad.

"Don't say that, Carson."

"I dislike Wes," Carson told his dad. "Intensely!" he added.

"Have you called Case or Gavin recently? Why not touch base with them in the morning."

"Last time we talked, Case said they were going camping together this weekend."

"Ah."

"In the mountains behind Pasadena. In an Airstream trailer."

"Ah."

Carson felt a twinge.

Did Gavin and Case even miss him?

Probably not that much.

They had each other to hang out with now.

Carson had no one to hang out with, and nothing new to report.

He had hoped to be able to tell them about a demolition derby.

Why call them at all?

10. GOOD-BYE,
Coop

On Sunday morning as Carson was playing tug-of-war with Genevieve, the phone rang.

Carson heard his dad say, "Yup, he is. Hang on a minute." His dad handed Carson the receiver, and Carson held on tight to the tug toy, with Genevieve growling on the end.

"Hello?"

"Hi, it's Patrick. Do you want to come with my mom and me to release Coop?"

Wow!

Did he ever!

"Sure! Can my dad come, too?"

Patrick spoke to his mom for a minute.

"My mom wants to talk to your dad."

The two parents hatched a plan to meet at the northern entrance to Green Gulch Park.

Carson and his dad drove up and parked. Patrick and his mom had just arrived and were walking to the middle of an open field, not far from where Coop had been found injured. Ms. Tapp was holding the Pet Taxi.

Coop was agitated, ruffled up and calling out.

"He senses freedom is finally near," Ms. Tapp told Carson and his dad. "Hi, I'm Ella." She took off one glove and offered her hand.

Carson's dad shook it. "Nick here. Great to meet you."

She set the carrier in the grass. "Okay, everyone, stand back a little." She put her glove back on. "Ready?"

Carson's dad turned on his camera. "Yup."

She carefully opened the door of the carrier and lifted Coop out with both hands. He gazed skyward.

Ella launched him into the air. Carson's dad documented the flight as Coop flew off, flapping his wings and landing in the top of a nearby pine.

Ella looked over at Carson and his dad. "My job never gets old."

"No, I don't imagine it would."

They chatted awhile about the rescue center; Ella wondered if Carson's dad might like to drop by the center and see what the organization was up to.

Maybe he'd even consider volunteering.

Carson and Patrick played catch with a dried-up pinecone while their parents talked.

They all headed back to the cars.

Carson's dad offered to treat at the International Yogurt Depot, and they met there for sundaes.

"Patrick is cool, isn't he, Dad?" Carson said when they got home.

"Yes, he is."

"And Ella is awesome, isn't she, Dad?"

"Yes, very."

"Have you ever seen anyone's mom order cheesecake yogurt with M&M's on top?"

"Never."

"I can't wait to email those Coop pictures! Do you think you got some good ones?"

Carson's dad handed the camera to Carson to preview the shots.

"Too bad Patrick got scraped off a horse's back and stung by a bunch of bees. Otherwise, I'd want to invite him and his mom on the trail ride."

"Well, you're supposed to get back on a horse again," said Carson's dad. "Once you fall off."

"Well, I don't think that's going to happen in the near future. But I'm thinking maybe Nancy and her mom might want to come."

"Who's Nancy?"

"A girl."

"Or I suppose there's always Eva and her aunt," said Carson's dad. "They seem nice."

"Do Eva and her aunt seem 'horsey' to you, Dad?"

"You can't judge by appearances. Does Nancy seem horsey?"

"Totally."

"What about her mom?"

"You can't tell by appearances. But I can tell you this much. Definitely an 'oh no!' on Weston Walker. *Anybody* but Wes Walker."

Carson slapped himself on the forehead. "I can't believe I fell for the demolition-derby whopper."

11. HELLO,
Buñuelos

The host at Mi Pueblo said the wait would be ten minutes, but the minutes were passing like hours.

"Dad. Would you ever consider babysitting Mr. Nibblenose? He's a very good boy. He is!"

"No! No rats. No rodents of any kind. *No!*"

"Sometimes you get a little bit grumpy when you're hungry, huh, Dad?"

"I'm sorry, son, but you know how I feel about rats. And with those horrible little yellow teeth." He made rat teeth at Carson.

"They don't have an opportunity to brush, Dad."

Carson strolled up to the white cement fountain

in the enclosed courtyard and counted up the coins resting on the bottom: four dollars and sixty-eight cents.

From where he was standing, near a large potted palm in a colorful ceramic pot, Carson noticed that— What?! Was that Mrs. Crabbly? It was! Wearing a wide-brimmed pink straw hat decorated with a big, fake purple marguerite daisy.

Carson decided to hide from her. To spy on her, truthfully. He slipped behind the potted palm, close to the wall. Then he parted two palm fronds and peered out. He saw two tiny LED lights blinking on her collar.

Carson observed Mrs. Crabbly buy a bag of *buñuelos*. She whirled around and looked directly at him. "I had a funny feeling I was being watched. What are you doing behind that tree?"

"Waiting for a booth," said Carson quietly.

Carson's dad offered his hand. "Nicholas Blum."

She shook it. "Abby Crabbly. Sorry about that darn crow incident."

"Oh well. That's the way the cookie crumbles," said Carson's dad.

"Well, that's one way of looking at it," said Mrs. Crabbly.

"But it did take me an hour to barbecue that tri-tip," he admitted.

"What's your marinade?"

"It's posted on my blog, *Gourmet Grub*."

"Have you blogged your way to Buster's Barbecue? It's just around the corner."

"In fact, we have."

"How 'bout them ranch beans, huh?"

Mrs. Crabbly untwisted the tie on the *buñuelos* bag. "Ever tried these?" She offered them to Carson and his dad and they each took one. "Bon appétit. See you at school, Carson." She lifted her hat from her head, put it back on again, and walked out.

"She seems like something of a character," Carson's dad said.

"You can say that again," said Carson.

"She seems like something of a character," Carson's dad said. "And what an unusual alien brooch," he added.

"What's a brooch?"

"A pin."

"She got that one from the Mystery Lights of Marfa gift shop in Marfa, Texas. She has a cuckoo clock from Switzerland also. And a legendary dog I've heard about, but haven't seen. She's funny! She reminds me of Grandma."

Through the glass door, Carson watched Mrs. Crabbly cross the street and head down the sidewalk. He liked Mrs. Crabbly and everything about her. He liked how grouchy she was with Wes.

He deserved it, the liar!

Carson savored the crispy, cinnamony, sugary *buñuelo*. He watched Mrs. Crabbly peer over a fence, then open a gate and stroll through. Maybe that's where Mrs. Crabbly lived. Maybe they were neighbors. In fact, of course they were neighbors because they had all walked to Mi Pueblo!

Carson dug into his pocket for a coin to throw in the fountain. *This will make it four seventy-eight*, he told himself. He wasn't great at math but he added money well. He threw a dime into the water and wished they could hurry up and sit down.

Bingo! It worked! Carson and his dad were seated in a bright blue-green booth by the window. Carson would have what he had last time: the *carne asada* burrito supreme. He'd eat half and ask the server to wrap the other half up in aluminum foil for tomorrow's lunch.

Yum!

His dad was examining the menu with his reading glasses perched on the end of his nose.

Carson slid his dad's shirt cuff up and looked at his watch. "It's six-forty-five, Dad. Let's order."

"Okay, okay. Let me think."

Carson watched a cop car pull to the curb. A very big, very wide, very tall officer in a dark blue uniform got out. He took off his sunglasses and gazed down the sidewalk.

"Have you signed up yet to come for Career Day and talk to the class about being a tax lawyer?" Carson asked his dad.

"I think so. I checked every box there was."

A server put a basket of warm tortilla chips in the middle of the table, and a small bowl of salsa. They ordered guacamole to go with the chips.

"I'll ask Mr. Lipman about setting a date."

A guy wearing a beautiful fancy black velvet

sombrero and pants with silver buttons on the sides strolled around the room, playing a guitar and singing.

"Is there a Wannabe Day?" asked Carson's dad. "Maybe I could come in and play my guitar and sing some oldies but goodies. Like 'La Bamba.'"

"La Bamba" was his dad's ringtone.

"I think Career Days are for actual jobs only. Time's a-tickin', Dad."

His dad looked at his watch and dabbed a small blob of guacamole off the face with one corner of his napkin.

Before long, Carson was staring at a white oval plate filled with creamy refried beans, crisp shredded lettuce, and a huge steamy burrito topped with sour cream. His dad had settled on *arroz con pollo*—a generous pile of chicken and tender mushrooms stuck together with melted white cheese on a bed of fluffy pink rice.

His dad shoveled a large bite in, held up five fingers, and said, "Five stars."

With his spoon, Carson cleaned off the sour cream he had plopped on the front of his hoodie. "I agree."

"I'll wash it, Carson. Ain't no biggie. Like father, like son, eh?"

"Thanks, Dad. It keeps shrinking in the dryer!"

"Well, maybe it's you getting bigger. Ever thought of that?"

Carson hadn't.

Eventually, Carson's dad sat back and suggested taking a breather.

"Want another Whiz Quiz clue?" Carson asked him.

"Okay, shoot."

Carson looked at his dad. "Braves caves."

"Braves caves? A bat?"

"No. Next: Air in its hair."

"Lion! Lion, king of beasts, standing on a ridge, in front of a cave, with its mane blowing in the wind."

Carson's dad waved to the musician and politely asked, "Do you know 'La Bamba'?"

They both loudly sang the song in Spanish.

Carson looked out the window. The patrol car was gone.

12. HELLO,
Star Jar

The next morning Carson sat quietly while Mr. Lipman took attendance and lunch count and read the announcements:

Principal's Update: Nuisance Bird

A large great horned owl decoy has been temporarily removed from the kindergarten garden and situated in the pine tree to discourage the Nuisance Bird from remaining in the area.

   If problems persist, there will be an immediate attempt by the Wildlife Rescue

Center to capture and relocate this unpleasant
and aggressive bird to a more appropriate
environment. Thank you to Patrick Tapp's
mother for the offer.

    Reminder: no food is to be left unsupervised
unless appropriately contained.

No worries. Carson's half a burrito supreme was in his new canvas lunch bag, along with an orange, a juice drink, and a few *buñuelos*.

Zipped up safe and sound.

Wes tipped sideways in his chair almost to the point of falling off. "I like the Nuisance Bird," he told Carson. "Do you? I'm not mad at him for dive-bombing me. He was just protecting his territory. FYI: I wasn't aiming to hit him with the pen—just scaring him off. It's my territory, too!"

Carson said nothing. He wanted to ask Wes where the heck he was on Saturday at six p.m. but didn't. He didn't want Wes to know they fell for his big fat whopper!

Wes continued: "Bob is a hungry old crow who has a botched-up beak and busted tail feathers and only one skinny, crooked leg to hop around on. He can't hop into a Porsche and drive down to the store to buy himself some candy bears."

"They're not candy bears. They're fruit bears."

"Well, whatever they are, that's what you get for leaving food out around wild animals. Never do that, and if you do—expect consequences."

"It wasn't my fault."

"Well, whose fault was it then?"

Carson didn't know the answer to that one.

"What's in your lunch today?" Wes asked.

"A burrito."

"No way! I love burritos! Anything else?"

"No!" Carson did not have a duty to divulge the contents of his lunch to Weston "the Whopper" Walker.

"Remember when I shared my sandwich with you the other day?" Wes asked.

"Wes?" said Mr. Lipman. "Shh!"

Wes whispered, "Want to trade hoodies?"

Carson ignored him.

"Squirrels give me the whim-whams. All rodents do." Then he whispered behind his hand, "That's why I hate Mr. Dribblenose."

A moment later he poked Carson's shoulder. "I can hardly wait for Star Jar. I hope my number gets picked because, oh boy, have I ever got a good story to share!"

Cody leaned close to Carson and said, "Whopper alert!"

"Mr. Lipman!" Wes called. "What about the New Kid's Star Jar stick? The New Kid doesn't have a number. And he probably wants to tell everybody about his dad's orange Porsche."

Matthew turned to him. "How would you know what Carson would talk about?"

"Well, *duh*. His name is *Car*-son. Isn't it?"

"What does that have to do with anything?"

"You like math, don't you, *Matth*-ew?"

Wes called to Mr. Lipman, "Do you like to skip?"

"I did when I was younger."

"I knew it. How old are you?" Wes asked.

"I'm thirty-eight, just about to turn thirty-nine."

"Whoa! You're pushin' forty!"

Mr. Lipman looked at him.

Then he pointed at the deputy list. "Numbers Deputy?"

"Yes?" said Nancy.

"Carson's number will be twenty."

"Okay."

Mr. Lipman took a large brown mug with a sunflower on it down from the shelf near his desk. It was filled with tongue depressors, one for each student in the class. He opened the bottom door of the cupboard near his desk and took a new tongue depressor from a package. He gave it to Nancy.

"Thank you. Now, where's the fine-point felt-tip marker?" Nancy asked.

Mr. Lipman looked in his top desk drawer. "Anybody seen it?" He opened the other drawers and rummaged through them.

Wes called to Cody, "Pssst! Cody! Do you like coats?"

"How about you shut your trap, Wes," Cody suggested.

Whoa! Good thing Mr. Lipman didn't hear *that*!

Shelly looked thoughtful. "Maybe there's something to Wes's theory. I like shells. I have a shell collection."

She asked Wes, "Do you like the Wild West, Weston?"

"Yup, I plan to be a rodeo clown."

"Oh wow," Cody mumbled. He turned to Matthew and held his fist with his thumb sticking up like a microphone. "Good afternoon, ladies and gents! Welcome to Weston's Wild West Whopper Show!"

When Cody and Matthew smirked, Carson looked away.

"Quick Writes," Mr. Lipman told the class. "Hop to it."

The topic of the day was "What I Want to Be When I Grow Up."

Mr. Lipman read over Carson's shoulder as he wrote, and so Carson wrote s-l-o-w-l-y and c-a-r-e-f-u-l-l-y and did the best possible job he could.

When I grow up, I want to be a veterinarian. I hope to attend the University of California, Davis. I hope to learn how to do surgeries such as removing foreign objects from the digestive systems of puppies. I would also like to be trained to deal with injured large wild animals such as moose and antelope and injured small wild animals such as gophers—on a volunteer basis.

Mr. Lipman asked Carson if he wanted to read his out loud, and Carson didn't, but he did anyway.

"Good job, Carson."

He turned to Wes and sighed. "Weston? I've told you this many, many times. Do not grunt and wave your hand in the air when someone else is reading or speaking unless it's an emergency."

"Sorry."

"Read."

Wes loudly read about wanting to be a rodeo clown and save bull riders who got tossed off a bull's back by distracting the bull and then jumping into a barrel and hiding.

"Good job, Weston. Next. Nancy?"

Nancy read, "'There are many things I am interested in, such as math and marine biology, and problem solving. I would possibly like to grow up to be a research scientist like my dad. However, I am not ruling out being a surgeon like my mom, a baseball player, or a detective like, you guessed it, Nancy Drew.'"

"Well done, Nancy."

"When's Star Jar?" Wes asked.

"Wes? Raise your hand before speaking."

Wes raised his hand. "When's Star Jar?"

"Look at the schedule."

At 9:28, Nancy handed Mr. Lipman a brand-new tongue depressor with 20 neatly written on it in fine-point felt-tip pen.

"Chloe and Zoe located your felt-tip pen. In the box in the cupboard along with the plastic eating utensils."

"Hmmm. What was it doing *there*?"

Chloe shrugged.

He stuck the number 20 in between the other sticks.

"Mix 'em up," Wes told him.

"Okay. Give us an intro, Wes."

Wes made a drumroll sound. Then a loud crash of cymbals, which Mr. Lipman hadn't requested.

"N-u-m-b-e-r . . ."

The class waited.

"Fourteen!" called Mr. Lipman.

"*Eeeeee-yes!*" Wes shouted. He jumped to his feet

and ran to the front of the room, his arms extended and his fists in the air.

"Brother," grumbled Sydney. "*Him* again. That guy got picked twice last week and now again. Some people never get picked. And Wes always seems to get picked."

"Sydney? The Complaint Department is closed."

"She's right, though. Zoe never gets picked," said Chloe. "She's never been picked once."

"Never? Not once?"

Zoe made a sad face and shook her head.

"That's strange . . . ," said Mr. Lipman.

"And actually, neither have I," said Chloe. She slyly looked at Zoe.

"You haven't?"

"Not recently."

Wes loudly sighed. "Can I start?"

Cody whispered to Carson, "Brace yourself for the biggest lie you've ever heard. Or one of 'em."

"O-kay, Wes. Let's hear it," said Mr. Lipman. "Remember: details. Build it up. Don't just tell the punch line."

"Last night . . . ," began Wes.

"Last night—when?" asked Mr. Lipman.

"About seven o'clock . . ."

"Where?"

"When we were driving on the freeway . . ."

"Who's we?" Mr. Lipman smiled at Wes. "I'm sorry, Wes. I'm sorry to interrupt. But I just want to make my point. Give plenty of details and build the story up. Go slowly. Capture the interest of your audience."

"O-kay," said Wes. "O-kay, here I go. Nice and slow. Last night . . . at about seven o'clock . . . when me and my grandma were driving on the freeway . . . I saw . . ."

His eyes got really big. "*Abby Crabbly riding in the back of a police car!*"

"What?"

"*Abby Crabbly riding in the back of a police car!*"

"You did not, and her name is *Mrs.* Crabbly."

"Yes I did! Mrs. Crabbly was riding in the back of a police car on the freeway in the fast lane."

"That's ridiculous," said Mr. Lipman. "You saw an individual who looked like Mrs. Crabbly—not the actual Mrs. Crabbly. End of story. Sit down."

"See what I mean?" Cody whispered to Carson.

Wes rambled on: "She was riding in the back of a police car and looking down. Looking guilty as anything. Like this." He looked down at the floor. "And I said, 'Gram! That's my computer teacher! Speed up!' I rolled down my window and yelled and waved. My grandma drove up close, right next to the patrol car, and blasted her horn!"

Mr. Lipman frowned. "Your grandmother blasted her horn at a police officer in a patrol car?"

"Yup, but Mrs. Crabbly just kept looking down at her lap."

"Wes?" said Mr. Lipman. "Sorry to say it: you're full of beans."

"Were her glasses on top of her head?" Eva asked. "With hair poking out?"

"Look. Enough is enough," said Mr. Lipman. "It may have been somebody who looked like Mrs. Crabbly, but was not Mrs. Abby Crabbly herself. Time's up. Have a seat. I mean it."

"Maybe Mrs. Crabbly has a sister," said Zach. "Who looks just like her. A twin. And maybe her twin sister embezzled money from a bank and was being carted off to the slammer."

"Zachary? Enough!"

Mr. Lipman pointed to the empty seat and Wes sat down.

He chose another tongue depressor from the Star Jar. "Number . . . fourteen?"

"Wahooo!" shouted Wes. "Me again!"

Mr. Lipman looked into the Star Jar. "How come there are two sticks with number fourteen on them?"

Wes said nothing.

"This calls for a stick check," announced Mr. Lipman.

He shook all of the tongue depressors out of the Star Jar. "Nancy?"

"Yes?"

"Take charge."

Nancy lined up the tongue depressors along the counter.

Mr. Lipman called Wes up to his desk and quietly talked to him.

Carson could hear the conversation.

"For some strange reason, there are two number fourteens in that jar. You know anything about this, mister?"

"Actually, three!" Nancy called out.

A moment later she added, "But no number one, and no number four."

"Who is number four?" asked Mr. Lipman.

Zoe raised her hand.

"No number four? None?" said Mr. Lipman.

"None," said Nancy.

"And no number one? Who is number one?"

Chloe raised her hand. "Me."

"Well, it appears as if a certain somebody threw away two tongue depressors and replaced them with his number. Completely unacceptable behavior. Weston? At lunch recess, you may stay in and tidy the room."

"Okay, but I didn't throw out any tongue sticks."

"Fine. Whatever you say. A little fairy did. I have no proof other than the fact that mysteriously there are three tongue depressors with your number on them. Stay in at lunch. Tidy the bookshelf and clean around the sink."

"Does this mean I'm Deputy Sink Scrubber?"

"For one day, yes."

"Will you write it on the board?"

"Fine."

"Can Carson be my honorary one-day Deputy Sink Assistant?"

"Does he want to?"

Wes asked, "Do you, Carson?"

Carson didn't want to. But he did want to demonstrate to Mr. Lipman that he was willing to work his way up from a low-level assistant position to Deputy Pet Care Giver.

"Uh . . . sure."

Wes took Carson aside. "And it's your turn to share your lunch with me."

"Where's *your* lunch?"

"I already ate it. During Quick Write."

Carson said, "Well, um. Well, I would but I only have one plastic fork!"

"No problem there." Weston took a white plastic eating utensil out of his back pocket and waved it in the air at Carson. "The fairies hooked me up!"

13. GOOD-BYE,
Buñuelos

The class filed behind Mrs. Crabbly into the computer lab.

"Why's everybody so quiet?" Mrs. Crabbly asked.

Nobody answered.

Wes called out, "Mrs. *Crabbly.* Do you like crab cakes?"

"What a question! Of course!" She strolled up and down the aisle, hands clasped behind her back. "No demo today. Add a slide about favorite animals to your PowerPoint presentation."

"Mrs. Crabbly," ventured Eva, "does your twin sister like crab cakes?"

Eva glanced at Zach and he popped his thumb up at her.

"What twin sister?"

"You don't have a twin?" asked Eva.

"No. May I continue? Carson—you'll be interested in this! Remember I saw you and your dad at Mi Pueblo? After I bought the *buñuelos*?"

Carson didn't mention that he had been monitoring her activity through the window by the booth.

"Well, right after that, on the way down the street, I saw a shrimpy little dog hardly bigger than a large rat racing down the sidewalk with its ears flying. He ducked under a fence.

"I went through a neighbor's gate to investigate. There he was: a pale tan teenie-weenie miniature Chihuahua backed into a corner, trembling and shuddering like this."

Mrs. Crabbly trembled and shook.

"I knocked on the door of the house and asked the owners to call the police, because the animal-control office was closed.

"I carefully approached the dog and put my hat over him. My hat moved around in the grass, then stopped. I peeked under. The dog was growling, and showing his gums and teeth at me. Actually, it sounded more like gargling than growling.

"So I put the hat back down. A moment later, I heard a little whimper. A sad little, pitiful little mournful sound. Heartbreaking, really."

Mrs. Crabbly looked at the students. "Never touch a stray dog. You may get bitten. Ask an adult for assistance."

"Go *on*!" cried Wes. "So then what?"

"Weston?" She peered over her glasses at Wes. "Let me pace my story the way I want."

Mrs. Crabbly was wearing her famous pooch brooch, a spotted flat puppy with an oversize head and a goofy expression. And a pointy tail that slowly wagged back and forth, back and forth, back and forth at the same time as its eyes slowly rolled back and forth, back and forth, back and forth.

"I carefully lifted the hat again. The Chihuahua had laid his ears back. His tail was tucked between little old legs. So I s-l-o-w-l-y picked up the hat completely and set it upside down on the lawn.

"Then I c-a-r-e-f-u-l-l-y lifted the Chihuahua into

my hat, and he curled up, shivering and shuddering. And looked at me like this."

She made a sad, sad scared face.

"A police officer showed up. The officer had no cage or box, and said he personally wasn't enthusiastic about small dogs. He said he had a key to the Humane Society's back entrance, and asked if I would be willing to drive there with the Chihuahua in my hat so we could put him in a cage overnight."

Mrs. Crabbly sighed. "It's against the law for me to sit in the front seat of a patrol car. So guess where I sat."

Weston stood up, raised his fists in the air in a triumphant gesture, and slowly turned around.

"Sit down, Weston. The dog was full of fleas. I just couldn't believe how many fleas were on that little old guy. I offered him part of a *buñuelo*, but he was too scared to eat.

"When I got home, I discovered several fleas hopping in my hat."

The children sat quietly. They were thinking about the little old dog in the cage. "What did you do with the fleas?" Shelly asked.

"I threw the hat out the door onto the lawn."

"Oh."

"Poor thing. We put him in a cage with dry kibble and water. If the owners don't come for him, the Humane Society will put him up for adoption. Hopefully, they'll find a loving adoptive family."

"Did he have a bed in the cage?" Shelly asked.

"No. I had to sacrifice my silk scarf from France."

"What color?" asked Eva.

"Multicolored. With pictures of boats."

Eva stared at her. "*Boats?* What kind of boats?"

"Sailboats. And if wearing a one hundred percent silk scarf made in Paris and silk-screened with Claude Monet sailboats is a fashion faux pas, then *ex-key-ooooose* me! I'm unfashionable. So what."

"I'm just making sure they weren't paddleboats."

"Paddleboats, sailboats, why would this concern you, Eva? They were sailboats, heeling. Anyway, if anyone knows of anyone interested in a Chihuahua, you might tell them there's a somewhat cute one at the Humane Society that could possibly come up for adoption in a week or less. Don't say old—say 'mature.' And never mind about the fleas."

After school, Carson waited for his dad to pull into the parking lot. He threw his canvas lunch bag into the car, climbed into the back, and buckled up. "Look in the pine tree, Dad. See it? A great horned owl moved in."

"Where?"

"Tricked you, Dad. It's a decoy hired to scare Bob away. Well, borrowed, actually."

"Ah. How was the burrito?"

"Fine. I only ate half of the half."

"Can I have the other half?"

"It's gone. Wes got it. He managed to somehow scramble up a white plastic spoon with three little pointy teeth on it. So I ended up having to share it with him."

"Ah. Any *buñuelos* left?"

"Are you kidding me? You put them in plain sight, right on top of the burrito!"

"Well, where else should I have put them? Under it?"

"I guess not. Dad? Can I ask you something?"

"What?"

"Can we adopt a Chihuahua if necessary?"

"Well, why would something like that be necessary?"

"Mrs. Crabbly says there's a Chihuahua at the Humane Society and he may end up needing a home. They try to find the owner, but sometimes they can't. He's a really really tiny little shrimpy pip-squeak and a very very good old guy. A little nervous. And barely bigger than Mr. Nibblenose. He has had to deal with quite a few fleas, so maybe that's why he's a jumpy boy."

"The size of a rat? Abby Crabbly would expect us to adopt a runty old jumpy Chihuahua—with fleas? How old is he?"

"Only if they can't find the owner! He's not old. He's mature. I'm sure the fleas have been taken care of."

"Tell Mrs. Crabbly I will be more than happy to contact the Humane Society and pay for a series of newspaper ads that will help reunite the dog with his owner."

Carson was quiet.

"He's all alone, Dad. Just sitting in a cage and shivering. And he's scared! When he's scared, he lays his little ears back like this." Carson held his hands backward, flat against his head.

"Well, what would Genevieve think?"

"Genevieve will love him. Genevieve will let him sleep with her in her basket. Genevieve loves all dogs—big or small, fat or thin, long hair or short hair, girls or boys, young or old. You know that, Dad."

At first, Carson's dad said nothing. "She might squash him. You know how she sits on Moose. She's not really aware of where her body is, her weight and so on."

"And he looks like this, Dad . . ."

Carson's dad glanced into the rearview mirror, and Carson made a sad, sad face.

His dad said, "Only if necessary. And I mean Absolutely. Positively. Necessary. Not to change the subject, but how's that security owl doing with keeping Bob in line?"

"So far, so good. Bob sat right beside her in the tree all day."

"Nice."

"Want another Whiz Quiz clue, Dad?"

"Okay, go."

"Floaty goatee."

"Floaty goatee? Hmmm. Floaty goatee . . . Ha!"

"What."

"Mountain goat crossing a river?"

"No. It has claws. Remember?"

"You didn't say that."

"Well, it does. It has twenty hard, sharp black claws. The same amount as a Chihuahua."

Carson frowned.

"What's up, son?"

"Nothing."

"Yes there is."

"Well, gosh, Dad. Think about it. There's a sad little elderly Chihuahua sitting in a cage at the animal shelter right now."

Carson's dad was quiet. "I'll give them the dough for the ad. Okay?"

"Fine."

"Not to change the subject again, but I scheduled an interview next week to meet and talk with the riding teacher about the trail ride."

"Thanks."

Next week was a long, long ways away. Would the lost Chihuahua still be sitting in a cage next week?

"She recommended you and I take one orientation lesson first. We learn about reading a horse's facial expressions, where to stand, how to mount, et cetera. She called me 'darlin'.'"

"Can a Chihuahua get bumblefoot from sitting in a wire cage?"

"Carson, I don't know what bumblefoot is."

"I read about it in the pet-rat book."

"Look. It's an animal shelter, Carson. Where they take excellent care of animals."

"Bumblefoot is from standing in a wire cage too much! Just one flimsy silk scarf to stand on, Dad. That's all Mrs. Crabbly left."

"I'm sure they supplemented that with a small blankie of some sort."

Carson hadn't talked to Case in a while. He called him up to tell him about the teeny-weeny Chihuahua.

Case listened. "Wow, that's sad."

"I know."

"I hope they find the owner."

"Me too."

Then Case told Carson that he and Gavin were going with their families to the Teenie Weenie Jelly

Beanie jelly-bean factory in about a week, and then on to play Peewee Golf.

That sounded like fun.

And Carson wished he could have gone with them.

However, he had work to do.

14. HELLO,
Dollie

Carson chose a Chihuahua book from the school library and read it for fifteen minutes every day during Sustained Silent Reading for four consecutive days. He needed to know as much as possible about the breed.

If the Chihuahua wasn't claimed by the owner within a few days, he would be offered to an appropriate adoptive home. What adoptive home would be more appropriate than Carson's? Plus, he would be an excellent play pal for Genevieve, who didn't have a single friend.

During Sustained Silent Reading, Carson learned

that Chihuahuas are intelligent and personable (but possessive); they get lonely easily, and some people place them in doggie day care while at work. Also, they are:

Comical.

Entertaining.

Quirky.

Loyal.

Eccentric.

Obsessive ear lickers.

Genevieve's ear flopped down, and that offered protection. Carson read on. Chihuahuas are best in pairs, and prefer Chihuahuas to other dogs.

There was a rap on the doorjamb of the classroom.

"Why, hello, Mrs. Walker. How can I help you?" said Mr. Lipman.

Carson looked up. Wes's grandma was standing in the doorway. "I decided to surprise everybody," she said with a wink. "Including the teacher. Hope you don't mind me springing this on you. . . ."

"Grandma!" yelled Wes. "What are you doing here?"

"Happy Phony Birthday, big guy!"

She strolled in. There was an airbrushed picture of a Buick LeSabre on the front of Wes's grandmother's shirt. On the back was an airbrushed picture of Wes! And PROUD GRANDMA printed above it!

She was carrying a big pink bakery box tied with white cotton string and a paper shopping bag with the tops of three two-liter plastic bottles poking out. A denim bag with a bump in the bottom was hanging from her arm. She put the box down on Carson's desk. She glanced down at his name tag, taped to his desk. "So you're Carson?"

"Yes, that's me."

"I'm Dollie Walker. Wes told me all about the orange 912. Now that's a sweet ride. And I understand you and your dad will be cruising it over to Wessie's For-Real Birthday Party on the twenty-second of August. Ever seen a grandma in a demolition derby?"

"No," said Carson.

She flashed a smile. "Well, get ready. Have you marked your calendar? Saturday, August twenty-second, six o'clock. Don't forget."

Carson played it cool. "We won't."

Saturday . . . *August* twenty-second? Why didn't

Wes tell Carson his birthday party at the track was months from now!

"Now, who all's ready for a cupcake! Wessie likes scary stuff, don't you, Wessie? Untie the string, Carson!"

Carson untied the string and carefully lifted the lid. Inside the box were two dozen cupcakes, each coated with thick white icing and artfully decorated to look like a bloodshot eyeball.

Awesome!

Wes's grandma began to pass them around. "Take the one you touch," she told the kids. "That's my rule. Right, Mr. Lipman?"

"Right."

"Nobody likes somebody else's grubby mitts on their food. And once you touch it, eat it. Right, Mr. Lipman?"

"Right."

"Mr. Lipman? Will you do the honors?"

She held up a two-liter bottle of orange soda.

Mr. Lipman began pouring the soft drink into the cups. "Actually, I'm supposed to point out to parents that we're limiting beverages with added sugar at school celebrations. . . ."

"Yes, I know, but I figured half a small paper cupful on a half birthday wouldn't be overdoing it. Pour everyone half a glass," she suggested. "And have half a belt yourself."

"Don't mind if I do."

Mr. Lipman poured himself a small swallow and drank it. "Where did you get the cupcake idea?"

"My ex-sister-in-law."

She added, "You should see her turkey cake. That's even better." She chuckled. "Her new husband's been threatening to arrest her if she bakes him a turkey birthday cake. He's a cop."

"I can't say as I blame him. A birthday cake made of turkey has *got* to be a criminal offense."

"Well, it's actually a chocolate cake baked and rearranged to be shaped like a turkey, iced with mocha frosting. And with squares of white cake for stuffing tumbling out from inside. And vanilla ice cream for mashed potatoes, and caramel syrup for gravy . . ."

"You're joking."

"Nope, I'm not. And strawberry sundae topping for cranberry sauce. It'll be a little hard to serve in the bleachers, but we'll figure it out."

The kids politely ate their cupcakes and sipped orange soda.

"So you have a police officer in the family?" Mr. Lipman asked.

"Yup, right here in town. And he told me next time I honk and wave at his patrol car on the freeway, he's going to pull me over and write me up."

"You honked at him on the freeway?"

"I have to admit it: Guilty as charged. Not a honk, though. More of a beep." Dollie laughed a little to herself. "I'm not going to do it anymore, though. He was mad as a hatter."

"Well, I must apologize to Weston then," said Mr. Lipman. "He told that to the class. To be honest, I thought he made it up. And said he was full of beans."

"Oh, that's okay. Don't worry about it. Sometimes he *is* full of beans."

Mr. Lipman asked, "Do you think your ex-sister-in-law's new husband would be willing to come in on Career Day? The kids would enjoy meeting someone in law enforcement."

"I'll ask—if he's still speaking to me. Clean up, Wessie," she told her grandson. "I gotta get outta here. Get to passin' the trash can around. Hop to it!"

Wow, thought Carson.

It was hard to sort through Wes's whoppers—hard to figure out fact from fiction. He wasn't always well behaved, that much Carson knew.

He'd forged tongue sticks and said he didn't.

But he wasn't telling a whopper about the turkey cake.

He had flat-out stolen a foroon from the cupboard and claimed that "fairies" gave it to him.

That was fiction.

Yet he wasn't telling a whopper about the demolition derby.

It was also a fact that Mrs. Crabbly *had* been spotted sitting in the back of a police car, and now—come to find out—Wes's grandma really had honked at a police officer! Or at least beeped at one.

Wes's grandma announced, "Okay, I guess I better go, but— Oops! I almost forgot!"

She took the tote bag off her arm.

There was an upside-down cat on the front. One rhinestone eyeball twinkled. "Everybody seen this bag Wes made me?" She held it up for the class. Nobody said anything about the cat being tail up. "But mercy me, what's this at the bottom?"

She peered inside. "Now, what have we here?" she said mysteriously, and slowly reached in. "Now, what's this down here at the v-e-r-y bottom of this b-e-a-u-t-i-f-u-l kitty tote my talented grandson made me at the community center?"

The class grew quiet.

They heard a faint gargling sound.

"Shh!" She gently lifted out a tiny little skinny scraggly scared Chihuahua with a black rhinestone-studded collar.

She told the Chihuahua, "Woof a Happy Phony Birthday to Wessie." And she handed him to Wes.

Wes just stood there, frozen. The Chihuahua's whiskers were trembling. His lips were twitching, then they rolled up and over his fangs.

Wes's grandma looked over at Mr. Lipman. "It's just a scare tactic, according to the canine shrink the shelter brought in to evaluate him. He's a scared pea-nut and it's all bravado. He wouldn't hurt a fly, really."

"Nonetheless, we do have a muzzle rule." Mr. Lipman looked through the top drawer of his desk and took out a shoelace. "He must be muzzled when visiting the school."

He gently tied the shoelace around the dog's nose.

Wes's grandma said, "That little pup's no spring chicken, Wessie, so you need to be real, real gentle with that guy."

Nobody had to tell Wes that. Wes was so gently holding the dog against his shirt. Just looking down at him, and the dog was just looking up at him, with his lips curled back and showing his teeth under the shoelace.

"Weston's wanted a dog all his life, but you know Wes," Dollie told Mr. Lipman. "We had a few goldfish, but, bless his heart, he kept overfeeding them. They looked like orange marbles. I had to give them away."

"Ah."

"But he was worried to death about this pooch after Mrs. Crabby told about him. Then I saw that nice ad about him in the paper. That was a flattering photo, I might add; they took it from his good side.

"I figured what the heck, why not. So I went on down and interviewed at the shelter to see if Wessie and me qualified as an adoptive family for a half-pint pooch."

"Ah."

"There was just me and a guy in a Porsche cap interested; he said he only wanted to be a backup." She called over, "Cute, isn't he, Wes?"

Then she said, "The shelter waited the minimum days. Then called me to come down and get him. Not that he isn't full of personality, but they said he wasn't highly adoptable at his age." She whispered, "And I don't think he'd win any beauty contests, either."

The Chihuahua pinned back his ears and licked Wes's nose.

"See? He's got a good heart. Just like Weston does. The dog acts tough because he's scared." She added, "Wes acts tough because he's tough."

She glanced over at Mr. Lipman. "Sure, Wes may get freaked out by rodents of various sorts, but he'll overcome that. And yes, he may have slept with ol' Captain Piano, all the way up until your last Stuffed Animal Day." She eyed Mr. Lipman. "But that doesn't mean Weston isn't tough as nails."

Dollie whistled quietly and looked out the window.

Mr. Lipman turned to Dollie and said, "Thank you for the eyeball cupcakes."

"No problem."

Then he asked in a low voice, "Captain Piano wouldn't be related to the rubber halibut that's in the June Box, would he?"

Dollie answered, "Eee-yup. He's a bass, actually."

"Wes slept with that thing every night?"

"Right on the pillow, right next to his head. With the Captain singing him to sleep with 'Down by the Bayou-oo-oo-oo'!"

"Are you joking?"

"We've had some long, quiet nights around our house since the Captain's been locked up—but Wes has adjusted. He just powers through."

Dollie said, "Wes loves fish and he loves to fish, just like his granddaddy did. I should find the time to take Wes fishing more often."

After a long moment, Mr. Lipman said, "Well, what the heck. Take the bass home then. The fish may not technically be stuffed, but I suppose sleeping with him every night would qualify him as stuffed for the purposes of Stuffed Animal Day. And I suppose I can overlook the scuffle he got involved in. I was told the stuffed killer whale provoked it."

Wes's grandma picked up Captain Piano out of the June Box. She blew a few ants out of his gills and shoved him into her tote. "I'm glad you see it my way."

The kids had gathered around Wes and the Chihuahua.

Eva was saying, "I have a fuchsia doll sweater with white heart-shaped buttons on the front at home that I think might fit him if you roll up the sleeves."

Carson strolled over.

"Okay," said Wes. "I think I'm going to name him Dandy. After my great-grandfather Daniel."

Dandy scrunched up his small, wet black nose and made the scariest face he could at Carson under the circumstances of the makeshift muzzle.

"Daniel's the one who figured out how to improve your chances of getting a date by using his Bad-Breath Pellets."

Maybe Daniel did and maybe Daniel didn't.

Who needed to know? Not Carson.

Carson had so much to tell his dad!

"Guess what, Dad! We got the demolition-derby date wrong. We went on the wrong twenty-second.

The demolition derby is on *August* twenty-second, which is Wes's For-Real Birthday. Can we still go?"

"You sure about that?"

"Positive. I got it right from the horse's mouth: his grandma. And she's bringing a turkey cake to the racetrack."

"I may pass on that."

"She adopted the lost Chihuahua for Wes."

"She did? Terrific!"

"That was you who went down there to check on the Chihuahua, wasn't it, Dad?"

"Yes." His dad paused. "They say that dog's only faking being a cranky, crotchety critter. But he could've fooled me! And he could use some dental work, I might add."

"Well, thanks for going down there, Dad. And giving money for the ad. And putting us on the backup list. How many names on it?"

"As far as I know, just us."

15. GOOD-BYE,
Mr. Nibblenose

"I absolutely positively simply can*not* understand how I got into this," Carson's dad told Carson when he picked him up.

"You got into it by filling out the parent volunteer sign-up sheet saying you would be happy to barbecue and play the guitar for a sing-along on the campout. And help make ceramic pinch pots or coil pots. Or participate in any other way that would help with the class. And so Mr. Lipman signed you up for barbecuer, campout sing-along song leader, pot pinching or coiling, and one of the many other ways that parents can help with the class: Nibblenose-sitting."

"I got on the rat list?"

"You're a lawyer, Dad. Don't sign anything without reading it first."

Carson's dad lifted the lid of the trunk.

"Okay. In goes Nibblynose."

"His surname is Nibblenose, Dad, not Nibblynose, and he can*not* ride in the trunk. A rat has to ride in the backseat."

"The cage won't fit in the backseat. In fact, the cage won't fit into the front seat or the trunk, either. Lookie here. This is a Porsche, not an SUV. I guess we better bring Mr. Nibbletoes back to Mr. Lipman."

"Mr. Nibble*nose* can sit in my lap in the backseat, Dad. We can attach the cage to the luggage rack with bungee cords."

"That, I'm afraid, would be against the law, unless we tie a red flag to it. The cage pokes out too far. It's against the California vehicle code."

"Your tie has red stripes. Would your tie qualify as a red flag?"

"Yes, I'm afraid it would. Wonderful. I will now proceed through the center of town with my tie flying like a flag from a rat cage attached to my luggage rack. With a tissue box rolling around in the bottom of it."

"Okay, thanks, Dad. And Mr. Nibblenose will sit safely in my lap. Just like the Chihuahua rode on Mrs. Crabbly's lap in the back of the police car. Actually, the Chihuahua was in a hat. Do you have your Porsche cap with you, Dad?"

"No, I do not. And if I did, I wouldn't volunteer it for a rat holder, and anyway, it'd never fit. Take a look at the size of that creature! It looks more like a possum than a rat!

"And may I add for the record: There is a physical barrier between the police officer who is driving the patrol car and the individual who is riding in the back of the patrol car. A thick plastic bulletproof division between the front seat and the passenger compartment, but in any event, get Mr. Dribblenose and get in."

Carson opened the door of the cage.

"Never lift a rat by the tail," Carson told his dad. He gently slid one hand under Mr. Nibblenose's belly and scooped him up.

"I have no plan to lift a rat by a tail or anything else in the foreseeable future."

"There we go," whispered Carson to Mr. Nibblenose.

He held Mr. Nibblenose against his chest. "See, Dad? Isn't he sleek?"

"Very sleek."

Carson watched as his dad attached the cage to the luggage rack.

"And he's a big guy!" said Carson. "Isn't he?"

"Yes he is. He's built like a linebacker. Now in we get. And hang on to him!"

Carson got into the back of the car. "Can you hold him for one minute just while I put on my seat belt?"

"I think you can manage," said his dad.

Carson put on his seat belt one-handed.

His dad buckled up and pulled out of the parking lot. "So where did Mr. Lipman get this beast?"

"A gift."

Carson held Mr. Nibblenose up so he could look out the window.

His dad batted at his left ear. "Did I just feel a whisker?"

Carson put Mr. Nibblenose back into his lap. "A neighbor of Mr. Lipman's named Belinda gave Mr. Nibblenose to the class as a present. Along with the cage, a water bottle, a ceramic food dish, food, Critter Litter. The works. Wasn't that generous?"

"Kindly keep that animal away from the driver."

"I am. Belinda moved to Belize to open up a bikini and boogie-board boutique near the beach. So she had to find him a good home. . . . And Mr. Lipman's class is a great home! Do we have any fruit in the house?"

"Yes. Fruit salad. And I'm happy you're looking forward to a healthy snack, because today I stopped at the farmers' market and bought locally grown organic fruits and cut them up in cubes."

"Do we have fresh veggies, too?"

"Yes! Thank you for asking. I also bought snap peas, celery, broccoli florets, cauliflower, and carrots. Check the fridge. A plastic bag full of crisp, colorful, cut-up veggies is waiting for you—with yogurt dip."

"Thanks, Dad."

"I even made cookies again after what the Nuisance Bird did to the last batch."

"Cool. Because along with his food block, Mr. Nibblenose likes fresh fruits and veggies. He also can eat yogurt, so thanks, Dad! But he can't eat cookies because sugary foods make rats hyper. He also likes cooked beans."

"I'm sorry to say I don't have any cooked beans. If Mr. Nibblenose is still hungry after fruit, vegetables, rat block, and yogurt, I suppose I can boil him up some beans. I aim to please."

Carson lifted Mr. Nibblenose and put him down again. "I estimate that he would weigh in at about . . . hmmm . . . maybe one pound. We'll weigh him on the bathroom scale when we get home."

"That will not be necessary," said Carson's dad. "Let's assume he's a one-pounder and leave it at that."

Carson's dad parked in the driveway and unhooked the cage from the rack and put his rumpled tie loosely around his neck. He carried the cage into the house and put it in Carson's room, on Carson's dresser.

He walked into the living room and watched at a distance as Carson let Mr. Nibblenose and Genevieve sniff noses. Carson put Mr. Nibblenose down on the rug. "You gotta see this!" He motioned his dad to come around the corner.

"Here, Mr. Nibblenose!" Carson called. "Come on, big guy!" He smiled at his dad. "Just watch. . . . Here, Mr. NibblenoseNibblenoseNibblenose! Watch! He'll come around the corner any minute."

They waited a minute.

"Hear him?"

They heard a tiny squeak.

"He's coming."

Carson's dad and Carson peered around the corner. Mr. Nibblenose was gone.

"Well, isn't this just a fine kettle of fish, Carson."

"Don't worry, Dad. The front door's shut and the back door's shut, so he can't get out."

"Well, hurry up and close my bedroom door!" said Carson's dad. "And make sure he's not in there first. I don't want a rat in bed with me!"

"Calm down, Dad. I already did. And there's no way he could have snuck past us and gotten all the way down the hall. And anyway, we'll find him before bedtime. He's just investigating the place. Rats are nosy critters, the rat book says."

Carson got a sinking feeling in his stomach. "Mr. Nibblenose is right here someplace. If you're worried, maybe it will help pass the time if you boil the beans and cool them," Carson suggested to his dad.

"I'm a private chef for a rat," mumbled Carson's dad. They went into the kitchen. Carson's dad began soaking some pinto beans. Carson put a small plate of fruit salad under the sink.

The beans had been sorted, rinsed, soaked, cooked, and cooled, and Mr. Nibblenose was still missing. "Rats are most active at dusk," Carson said. "I'm sure we'll hear him fiddling with something."

Where could he be? What would the kids in the class say if Carson lost him? What would Patrick say?

Carson's heart really, really went through the floor when he thought about this: How would Mr. Nibblenose feel, lost and alone?

Carson and his dad quietly ate dinner. Carson said no thanks to the sorbet and berries for dessert.

"Are you serious?"

Carson was. "I'm full, Dad."

But the truth was, Carson didn't feel like he deserved dessert, after losing Mr. Nibblenose.

When they had done the dishes and were reading in the living room, Carson's dad closed the newspaper and said, "Maybe Genevieve can sniff him out."

Carson let Genevieve get a whiff inside the Fluff Puff box. The box got stuck on her nose, but Carson pulled it off. "Go get 'im, girl!"

Sniffing the ground, she hurried into the kitchen, her tail wagging.

"See? She's onto him!"

Genevieve found the dish of fruit salad and ate it. "I have never known another dog that likes kiwis," Carson's dad told Carson.

Well, at least we have the whole long weekend to find him, Carson thought. But when he went to bed that night, he just lay there, staring up at the dark ceiling. Like Moose. Eyes wide open. He was listening— listening for the sound of tiny teeth chomping on something. He was listening for the sound of rustling paper. Of little scampering rat feet, if it was possible to hear such a sound as that.

But all he heard was the faint sound of his dad snoring in his room down the hall, with the door shut and a towel stuffed under the door.

Until . . . what was that?

Carson heard a squeaking noise.

He jumped up and hurried into the kitchen.

The squeaking noise was coming from behind Genevieve's basket!

He could hear it.

Squeeeeak.

Pause.

Squeeeeak.

Pause.

Squeeeeak.

Pause.

Never mind.

It was Genevieve's nose.

Carson went back to bed and fell asleep.

At dawn, his dad appeared in the doorway wearing pajamas with pictures of baseballs on them. "Carson?"

"What?"

Carson sat up.

"Come listen outside my closet door."

Carson and his dad walked quietly to the closet door.

It was silent.

Then he heard it—the distinct, distant, muffled sound of rustling paper.

Carson opened the door. But all he could make out in the dark closet was a row of shoes, neatly lined up, and a bootjack.

And, way in the back, the Dan Post cowboy boots.

One was tipped over. "I wish I could see better," Carson said.

Carson's dad found his key ring with a penlight on it. "Here. Squeeze this."

Carson crawled into the closet and shone the penlight inside the boot. There was a big pile of shredded tissue paper inside, and it was moving.

In the center, Carson could see the pink end of Mr. Nibblenose's nose and his two itty-bitty nostrils at the very tip!

"Yay!" cried Carson. "We found you!"

Carson crept closer. Suddenly he backed out of the closet and looked up at his dad. "You've got to see this to believe it, Dad."

"Just tell me. What?"

"You have to look, Dad. You have to see for yourself."

"Okay. Give me the light." He pinched it a few times and it went on and off.

"Okay, Nicholas, you can do this!" he told himself.

Then he got down on his knees and cautiously approached the boot.

Mr. Nibblenose squeaked at him and he jumped back.

Carson's dad stood up and Carson closed the door.

"I'm not sure how happy Mr. Lipman is going to be with a bootful of bald baby rats," said Carson's dad.

"I'm sure they'll grow hair eventually," Carson told him.

16. HELLO,
Mrs. Nibblenose

"What am I going to do with a closetful of runty rodents?"

"Squatters' rights, Dad!"

"Nonsense!"

"Plus, they're too delicate to pick up yet. They're like puffy, soft, four-legged beige caterpillars!"

"Stop. You're making me woozy just thinking about it, and squatters' rights nothing!" Carson's dad declared, hands on his hips. "I want that boot out of my closet and installed in the rat cage, and the rat cage and its contents returned to Mr. Lipman. Pronto!"

"Install a cowboy boot in a rat cage? Will it fit?"

"You bet your boots it will. I'll make it fit!"

He stormed out of the room and into the garage. Carson heard some banging and clattering.

The *Caring for Your Pet Rat* book cautioned that mama rats can be protective of their young, but Mrs. Nibblenose seemed quite delighted to be out and about with Carson and Genevieve, nibbling kibble, during the half hour it took his dad to modify the cage door wider with wire cutters and c-a-r-e-f-u-l-l-y navigate the cowboy boot full of ratlets out of the closet and into the cage.

Carson's dad called, "Okay, Carson! Bring her on!"

Carson's dad had put the cage in the guest room on the dresser near a window. The curtains were drawn, because Carson's dad suspected Mrs. Nibblenose would prefer the dark.

He stood at a distance while Carson carried her in.

Mrs. Nibblenose hurried through the cage door and hopped into the boot to check her babies.

That done, she hopped back out again and took a long drink from the water bottle.

"Okay. Monday morning and the whole clan is outta here!"

"Fine."

Carson looked at the cage.

"How will we move it?"

Carson's dad frowned. "You got me."

"That's okay, Dad. I don't think we'll be able to bring a cage with a bootful of bald Nibblenoses back to the classroom right away anyway. Do you?"

"Of course we will. Why wouldn't we? I'll rent a van if necessary."

"Mama rats get stressed out about people looking at their pups. I think Mrs. Nibblenose will be happier right here for a while, don't you? Right here in the guest room?"

"What pups?"

"Baby rats are called pups, and mama rats are called does, and if we're going to have rats around for a few weeks, I think we should use the proper terminology."

"A few *weeks*? *Are you kidding me*? The puppies will be safely hidden in a huge, soft, fluffy pile of shredded white tissue paper in a boot with hand-tooled leather tops high enough to protect a wrangler's legs from thorny desert brush. No one can see in there. No one!"

"When you go around to the other side of the cage, you can look in at them. See for yourself."

Carson's dad heaved a huge sigh. "This calls for a professional consult. Where's the paper with the phone tree on it?"

Carson's dad called Ms. Tapp, and she and Patrick came straight over.

"Yee-haw!" cried Ella. "Love the boot concept! What a novel idea for a nest! They'll be very, very happy campers in there for a few weeks."

"Thank you."

"Of course, the pups will need to be socialized in order to get them ready for adoption."

"Of course."

"So starting at, say, about day five, they'll need to be handled gently every day."

Carson's dad pinched his forehead and looked at the floor. "Wow. That's a tall order. I don't actually usually socialize with rodents, to be honest."

"Patrick and I can come over and start you off if you like."

"Thanks."

"Of course, this situation is Mr. Lipman's responsibility, not yours, Nick."

"Thank you for reminding me of that."

"He'll have to find adoptive homes, and place the pups in advance. But I think he'll appreciate our help. Patrick and I will be out of town for a family reunion on Carnival Day weekend, unfortunately, but maybe we can get things ready in advance, and you and Carson can set up an informational table for potential adoptive families."

"Good idea."

Carson and Patrick walked into the classroom together. "Boys? What's up? You look like you swallowed a cat."

"You tell 'im," Carson told Patrick. They shared the astounding Nibblenose news with Mr. Lipman.

Carson added, "My dad wants you to call him."

"Yes, I'm sure he does!"

"Leave it to Belinda," he mumbled. "Good gravy. What a shock!" He ran his fingers through the top of his hair. "I'm going to let you tell the class."

Mr. Lipman rang the chimes. Patrick waited for the class to be completely quiet. "Well," he began. "It's about Mr. Nibblenose . . ."

Wes lifted his desktop, stuck his head inside, and roared, "Aaaaahhhh-choo!"

He slammed the lid closed.

"My word, Weston," said Mr. Lipman. "What's going on?"

"I didn't have time to cover my sneeze so I aimed the germs into my desk. They're trapped in there now. I might be allergic to Dandy's doggie dander."

"Get tissues and use the hand sanitizer, Weston."

Nancy raised her hand. "Is 'achoo' an onomatopoeia?"

"Yes."

She put it at the top of her list.

"Is 'sneeze' an onomatopoeia?"

"Affirmative."

"Thanks."

Patrick cleared his throat.

"I'm sorry, boys," said Mr. Lipman. "Carry on."

Patrick announced, "As it turns out, Mr. Nibblenose is not a buck."

The class stared at him.

"Mr. Nibblenose is a doe."

The class still stared at him.

"A buck is a boy. A doe is a girl."

The class still stared at him.

"Mr. Nibblenose is a Mrs. Nibblenose. And Mrs. Nibblenose had fifteen babies at Carson's house that are now temporarily housed in a boot inside of a cage."

Matthew said, "What?!"

And Shelly yelled, "Whoopee! We'll have sixteen class rats!"

"Calm down. No, we won't. We can't!" cried Mr. Lipman.

"Yay! Fifteen baby rats!" the kids cheered.

Chloe and Zoe linked elbows and began dancing. "Wheeee!"

"Can we come over and see them?" several kids asked. "Can we, Carson? Huh?"

"Um . . ."

"Let's have a baby-rat shower," suggested Shelly. "A pup shower! And each person bring fifteen rat toys! Or one big toy that all fifteen pups can share!"

She ran over and began to leaf through the *Caring*

for Your Pet Rat book. She held up a page with a photograph of a carton full of sand and buried treats. "Anybody want to help me make an I Can Dig It Box?"

"We doooooo!" called Zoe and Chloe.

Patrick and Ella came back over after school in Ella's van. They brought boxes of all sizes, masking tape, a drop cloth, and some wide plastic pipe. They brought some brand-new cardboard cartons, still folded, and some jumbo binder clips.

Patrick brought a pair of his uniform pants from the second grade that he found in the bottom of his closet.

They brought a paint-roller pan to make a shallow wading pool.

Working together in the guest room, Patrick, Carson, Carson's dad, and Ella constructed a Free-Range Roaming Rat Arena for Mrs. Nibblenose and for the ratlets, once they were big enough to be out and about.

The Free-Range Roaming Rat Arena consisted of a plastic drop cloth on the floor with a freestanding cardboard corral around it.

Inside, several boxes with doors and windows cut into them were taped together to make a clubhouse. Ella created with segments of plastic PVC pipe some tube slides that came out of the windows so that doe and pups could slide from the clubhouse to the floor.

They also positioned rocks from the garden so that the rats could jump happily from rock to rock, and then up onto a small maple branch, which Carson had found by the rock wall.

Carson's dad got into the act. He cut his Nor Cal T-shirt into strips. "It was only the price of a card," he explained to Ella. Plus, he didn't look that good in fluorescent green. He knotted the strips into a climbing rope.

Patrick made a hammock from one leg of his uniform pants.

"That should do it for now," Ella said.

Carson's dad provided some snacks, and everyone sat at the kitchen table and devoured them. The boys went out to play catch in the yard, but Genevieve interfered with the game.

Ella and Carson's dad studied the Carnival Countdown announcement:

CARNIVAL COUNTDOWN!
COME TO CARNIVAL DAY!
BRING YOUR FAMILY & FRIENDS AND JOIN THE #1
SOCIAL EVENT AT VALLEY OAK ELEMENTARY SCHOOL!
FUN, FOOD, FAMILY!
PRESALE TICKETS ON SALE SOON!
GIANT SLIDE, CAKE WALK,
INFORMATIONAL BOOTHS, GAMES, FACE PAINTING,
RAFFLE,
COOL STUFF, AND PRIZES GALORE!
HOT DOGS, PIZZA, TACOS, COTTON CANDY,
SNO-CONES, PULLED-PORK SANDWICHES, AND MORE!
STUDENTS, WANT TO SIGN UP TO WORK IN A BOOTH?
SIGN-UP SHEET IS IN THE OFFICE.
DONATIONS FOR THE RAFFLE PRIZES GRATEFULLY
ACCEPTED. PLEASE LEAVE WITH MRS. SWEETOW
IN THE OFFICE.

17. HELLO,
Carnival Day

It wasn't easy to take a close-up digital photo of every single rat pup, assign a name to each one, and print out every photo with the pup's name attractively positioned underneath it.

But they had plenty of help from Patrick and Ella Tapp, who came over several times after day five to help socialize the ratlets.

Carson's dad wasn't ready for a lovefest with the baby rats, but he did have a flair for pup portraiture.

Carson and Patrick each took turns holding a pup in the palm of his hand while Carson's dad zoomed in, careful to get a flattering shot of each one, which wasn't difficult.

They were all so cute!

Carson really wished he could keep the white one with the perfect bow-shaped black marking. They named it Bosen Nibblenose: Bo for short.

After that black bow tie!

So stylin'!

The bow-tie shape would have been better under Bo's neck than on the side of Bo's head but still looked great!

Patrick and Carson researched information about the proper care of rats and how much fun they were to own. Patrick's mom helped them write up the information.

They worked in Photoshop to design an attractive foldable brochure with Mrs. Nibblenose on the front, surrounded by her large litter.

When Carnival Day arrived, Carson and his dad showed up early and set up a card table with a sign that said:

ADORABLE RAT PUPS!
SOON TO BE ADOPTABLE!
RESERVE YOURS NOW!
INFORMATION AVAILABLE HERE.

Before setting up the table, they bought twenty twenty-five-cent raffle tickets from Ms. Pierson at the entrance.

"Thank you so much for taking on this project with the rat adoption," she told Carson's dad. "Very, very appreciated, I can assure you." She rolled her eyes. "Jeepers creepers. Guess Skip Lipman will think twice before accepting any more classroom pets from people leaving the country."

After they set up the table, Carson's dad gave him five one-dollar bills to spend and then sat down at the table with his Porsche cap on crooked while Carson prowled around the carnival.

The five bucks was burning a hole in Carson's pocket. He bought three tickets for the rubber-ducky pond in hopes of netting the rubber ducky with the gold star on the bottom. Ms. Parker was in charge of that one. If you got the gold-star rubber ducky, you could take your pick of prizes!

He gave Mr. Lipman one dollar for a tangerine-flavored sno-cone. His lips would turn orange, but he probably wouldn't run into Nancy. She told him she wasn't coming till the afternoon.

Mrs. Crabbly and Mrs. Sweetow were in charge of a booth Mrs. Sweetow constructed, where you tried to shoot a marshmallow through a hole in a piece of plywood with a slingshot. There were branches stapled to the plywood and a few beanbag squirrels in the branches with their mouths open and ratty tails. The sign above it said SQUIRREL STASH.

Mrs. Sweetow and Mrs. Crabbly were sitting in folding metal chairs, chatting.

Out of the corner of his eye, Carson saw Mrs. Crabbly's squirrel pin, flicking its fuzzy tail and then chattering its teeth.

Shelly and Sydney were taking tickets and helping manage the booth. "Have you seen Weston?" Sydney called. "He signed up to help us."

"No, I haven't."

"So far, he's a no-show," said Sydney.

A kid with the slingshot walked up close to the shooting line and misfired.

The marshmallow hit one of the toy squirrels, which fell off the branch and flopped onto the ground.

Mrs. Sweetow picked it up and put it back on a branch. "Get up there, you."

"Not sure, but maybe he's not showing up," said Shelly, "because squirrels creep him out."

Mrs. Crabbly looked over. "They do? What's not to like about a squirrel?"

The beanbag squirrel plopped onto the ground again, landing on its back.

Everyone was quiet.

Carson checked out the Lily Pad Leap, where you tried to toss a rubber frog completely onto a large green paper lily pad without its legs hanging off.

He could have dominated that game but didn't play because he was saving his last dollar for more important things: He snuck up on his dad with a pulled-pork sandwich.

"Watch out for drips!" he cautioned. But so what if his dad was messy sometimes? What other dad would sign up to sit at a card table for four and a half hours trying to locate responsible potential owners for baby rats?

People were already flocking to the table. Well, not flocking maybe, but already one interested party had come up to the rat table with her kid and had begun to browse through the rat portraits. "You promise you will help feed and care for it?" the mom was asking her daughter, who was nodding her head to everything. "And help clean the cage, and put fresh water in the bottle? Look at this little guy! Bo. That's a cute name! And it has a bow, too! Like a little bow tie, but in the wrong place! Isn't that one adorable?"

The little girl nodded enthusiastically!

"Shall that be the one we choose?"

"Oh . . . I'm sorry," said Carson's dad before the kid had a chance to answer.

He glanced at Carson. "That one's already been spoken for."

The mom and daughter selected their second favorite, and the mom gave Carson's dad her contact information.

"But only just Bo," he told Carson after they walked away. "And nobody else. Not any more. I mean it, mister."

Over the course of the next couple of hours, many families came to the adoption-information table, including several of Carson's classmates and a few kids from Ms. Parker's class.

Before the end of the carnival, seven families had

signed up for adoption, and of the seven families, four were taking two.

How lucky could Carson get?

He would be keeping Bo. Bo might enjoy a play pal.

He'd bring that up later.

Well, as it turned out, even luckier! He got the ducky with a gold star and won a raffle prize!

"How did I end up with a plug-in fake aquarium with phony fish in it?" Carson's dad mumbled to himself as he and Carson headed to the car.

"Dollie contributed it. Put it in the guest room, Dad. Grandma and Grandpa like tropical fish!"

"These aren't fish! They're cardboard impostors! Covered with paper and glitter!"

"Well, we won't have to buy fish food for them. Or clean the tank."

"I guess that's a point."

"Can we get some real fish sometime?"

"That's a maybe."

"Can we go fishing at the pond sometime? When Grandma and Grandpa come?"

"You betcha."

"Did I tell you Wes sleeps with a rubber bass screwed onto a board?"

"It's screwed onto an actual board?"

"Yup."

"Soft or hard rubber bass?"

"Medium."

Carson's dad took off his Porsche cap and scratched the top of his head. "Wow." He put his hat back on and stared at Carson, from under the brim.

"There's one small maroonish-brownish barbecue-sauce thumbprint under the bill of your hat, Dad."

"There is?"

"Did you tip your hat hello to someone when you were eating?"

"I don't recall."

"How about after you were done?"

"Yes, I guess I did say hello to Eva's aunt."

"Will she be taking a rat?"

"I'm working on it."

18. HELLO,
Stuffed Animal Day

Nancy reminded Carson: "Stuffed Animal Day is coming up, Carson."

Carson said he didn't have a stuffed animal.

Nancy said, "Yes you do. What is it?"

She crossed her arms on her chest and then drummed her fingers near her elbow. "Come on. Spit it out."

It was hard to lie with a straight face. "I'm serious! I don't have one, I don't!"

Whatever Moose was, wasn't actually that easy to determine just by looking at him.

To begin with, his ears were bald. Carson had

concentrated on petting them quite a bit when he was young.

Then there was an issue with his antlers. There weren't any. When Genevieve was a puppy, she got out of her crate one afternoon when Carson and his dad were grocery shopping.

The door hadn't been properly latched.

When Carson and his dad returned, Genevieve was sitting in the crate, with the door wide open.

She was just lying quietly with her small dry nose resting between her paws, looking up at them.

At first, they didn't know what was wrong.

Then they discovered the rumpled bedspread, sheets, and blankets.

And Moose, lying under the bathroom sink.

They saw the extent of his injuries. Apparently, Genevieve had burrowed under the covers where Moose was sleeping and damaged his tail quite a bit—she ate the tip off it.

She also consumed both antlers.

She devoured his dewlap: the floppy flap of cloth dangling from the front of his neck. Stuffing was coming out.

Off they all went to the Pasadena Animal Hospital. Dr. Tichenal took X-rays of Genevieve and admitted her for observation.

Carson sat Moose up on the counter in the waiting room next to a WELCOME sign.

Dr. Tichenal came out and quietly spoke with Carson's dad about Genevieve's situation.

Then he listened carefully to Moose's heart and said Moose sounded good and told Carson that the missing antlers shouldn't pose a problem. A moose sheds its antlers every year, anyway. And grows a new rack in the spring.

As for the dewlap, he could do without it. It didn't serve a critical function. He was just as good-lookin' without it.

Dr. Tichenal poked the stuffing back in and stitched closed the opening in Moose's neck, stitched up the antler holes, and cropped and repaired the tail.

Carson asked, "Will Moose grow new antlers?"

Dr. Tichenal was honest: "Under this particular set of circumstances, I doubt it."

He gave Carson a business card from a card holder. It said *Robert Tichenal, DVM* and had a small picture of a dalmatian jumping over the letters with its tongue hanging out and its ears blown back.

"If you have any further questions or concerns about the moose, feel free to give me a call."

They went home without Genevieve.

For two weeks after her stomach surgery, Genevieve had to wear a white plastic collar that looked like a satellite dish so she wouldn't lick the surgery site. She walked backward around the house bonking into the furniture, but afterward she was fine. Good as new.

And five years later, Genevieve still was good as new.

Yay for Dr. Tichenal!

The best veterinarian in the world.

Carson put his hand on top of Genevieve's head and then fiddled with her silky left ear. "Thank you, Dr. Titch," he whispered.

Carson knew that not every veterinarian could so skillfully remove antlers from the belly of a puppy or would or listen so attentively for a heartbeat inside a stuffed animal that some scared little kid brought in, but he planned to be one of them.

Carson and Genevieve stood at the living room window, side by side, watching the huge raindrops plop onto the shiny deep-green leaves of the rhododendron plant on the other side of the windowpane. He opened the front door and they looked out. They breathed the cool, dark, damp fresh air. The wind lifted and tossed the branches in the yard. The trees in the distance were still black against the sky, but silver light was filling the air.

Thunder rolled.

His dad appeared behind them. "Would either of you like a cup of hot chocolate?"

"I would! Thanks, Dad."

"Would either of you like a dog biscuit?"

Genevieve knew a little English.

She woofed.

A cup of hot chocolate did sound good, with a little puff of whipped cream on top.

Soon Carson and his dad were relaxing on the front porch on wicker chairs with flowered cushions, drinking hot chocolate and watching the rain gently falling past the motion light onto the dark lawn.

Genevieve was sitting at attention on the porch boards, head up and tongue out.

The biscuit was long gone.

She was on a leash, the loop trapped under a chair leg, because you never know about a dog and thunder.

It like smelled Montessori school, in the rain. Maybe it was the flowering azalea bushes. Raindrops were pooling in the petals. Carson thought of the honeysuckle bushes that grew on the fence around the Rainbow Ridge yard, where he harvested blossoms in the springtime and drank the nectar.

Well, he didn't exactly drink the nectar. He pinched it out of the bottom of each white flower, just one small, clear drop. Barely a taste. But it tasted great, and he had the funny feeling that from now on, for the rest of his life, whenever he tasted honeysuckle, it would remind him of Rainbow Ridge. And when he was reminded of Rainbow Ridge, he would always miss it.

Always.

"Tomorrow's Stuffed Animal Day," Carson told his dad.

"Are you bringing Moose?"

"No, Dad."

"Why not? It's okay if he's worn out. It's fine to

bring him, I think. There's a wonderful tradition of kids and worn-out stuffed animals. Remember *The Velveteen Rabbit?*"

"Yeah."

"How the old rabbit ended up becoming real and hopping off with the other real rabbits?"

"That's the saddest story in the world, Dad."

"Right."

Little streams of water were running over the stone path. The trees were dripping water onto the ground. Wind was blowing rain up onto the porch.

"I guess we better go in," said Carson's dad. He picked up Genevieve's leash. "Grab a cushion."

Carson stood for a minute outside, watching the wind swirl in the highest branches. Before long, he and Moose would both be nine.

That night, Carson had a dream:

He was riding on Moose's back, and they were galloping in the rain. Carson's Valley Oak hoodie hood had blown back, and rain was splashing on Carson's face and Carson loved it!

Moose was young and strong. He had grown a fresh

dewlap and a new rack of antlers, and they were covered with brown velvet. He had two brand-new ears, and Carson leaned forward and whispered into one of them, "Let's go!"

Suddenly Moose reared up.

He could fly!

They flew high up into the air, over buildings and houses. Down below, Carson could see Nancy, laughing and swimming in a frothy turquoise swimming pool with Ethel.

She waved to him.

"Come down and swim with us!"

Carson woke up. It was morning.

Moose was staring straight at him from across the pillow.

Carson's Valley Oak uniform was folded neatly on top of his dresser, with the sweatshirt on top. His dad was such a great dad! He had washed and dried the hoodie yet one more time, and soon it would be too small, but oh well.

Carson called to his dad, "I've decided to take Moose to Stuffed Animal Day."

Carson got dressed and walked into the kitchen.

"Good decision. I was afraid he'd try to follow you if you didn't!"

"But I'm going to leave him in my backpack."

"Fine."

Carson ate oatmeal with brown sugar, raisins, and a few blueberries on top, had a small glass of orange juice, and took one kid-size vitamin.

"Thanks for washing all my stuff, Dad."

"No problem. That hoodie's shrinking so fast, and you're getting bigger so fast," his dad said. "I may stop by the office and buy a bigger hoodie from Mrs. Sweetow."

"Okay, but she's been in a pretty bad mood lately, I'm warning you."

There wasn't much in Carson's pack, so there was plenty of room for Moose. He carefully lifted him in.

You're ridiculous, Carson told himself. But he left the zipper unzipped a little so Moose could breathe properly and look out.

His hoodie would have crowded Moose if he had crammed it into the backpack, and he didn't feel like wearing it, so he casually threw it over one shoulder and headed down the porch steps, holding his canvas lunch bag while his dad locked the door.

He called to Carson, "Should we put in some lawn clippings for Moose to munch for lunch?" He chuckled softly to himself.

"Negative on that, Dad."

19. GOOD-BYE,
Moose

The schoolyard was full of kids strolling around with their stuffed animals, gathered in groups with their stuffed animals, giving their stuffed animals turns on the slide. Cody was tossing his stuffed killer whale through the basketball hoop.

Carson set his sweatshirt on top of the heap of sweatshirts and packs that were plopped on the ground near his classroom door. He thought better of taking off his pack. Wes was standing nearby, talking to Oswaldo and Patrick. "Did you bring stuffed animals?" Wes asked them.

They both said, "Nah."

Carson kept his mouth shut.

Wes said, "Me either. I'm not taking any chances on losing Captain Piano." He frowned in Cody's direction.

Carson heard someone calling his name in a tiny little high voice. "Howdy there, Carson!"

Carson looked over at Nancy, and she was holding one of Ethel's worn-out black leather paws and waving it at him.

"Did you bring somebody to hang out with me today?" Ethel squeaked.

Carson hid a smile. He ran off and played soccer awhile with Oswaldo, Wes, and Patrick. "How come you got your pack on?" Wes called to Carson.

Before Carson could think up a good excuse, the bell rang and everyone went to their classrooms.

The kids were allowed to perch their animals on their desktops or sit on their chairs with them.

The classroom looked like a zoo.

Carson left Moose in his backpack, which he hung on the hook in Mr. Lipman's class. He thought about bringing his pack to Ms. Parker's room for Math Switcheroo, especially because Wes had been wandering around the room aimlessly, stopping occasionally to look into the June Box.

Don't be ridiculous, Carson chided himself.

He walked across with a small herd of Mr. Lipman's students: Oswaldo, Luciana, Nancy, Matthew, Sydney, and Patrick.

"Welcome, welcome!" Ms. Parker called to them. "And welcome to all your animal pals as well. I hope they won't be too noisy in math. No animal today, Carson?"

"Nope."

"Be good at Mr. Lipman's!" she warned her departing students as they carried their stuffed animals out the door toward Mr. Lipman's classroom.

"And, Parks?"

"Yeah?"

"Don't forget to give Mr. Lipman the note so he knows you're supposed to be excused early for your Tahoe trip."

"I won't."

"Poor kid!" she said behind her hand. "Has to go to Tahoe for the weekend."

"Please accept my sincere sympathy," she called to

Parks. "That's a rough job, up there snowboarding in fresh powder!"

Parks smiled a little.

"Got your homework packet, Parks? Oh, that's right. You've been saving your No-Homework Pass— good thinking. Got your trumpet? Good thing you cleaned out your pack. Is that where you found that pack rat? Oh, sorry, Parks! That's not a pack rat parked on your hat. It's a kangaroo rat roosting on your hat. Can you carry all that okay?"

Ms. Parker giggled at her own jokes as Parks walked out. His arms were full: hoodie, pack, and trumpet case. He was wearing a baseball cap with a kangaroo rat attached to the top—hanging on for dear life.

Ms. Parker addressed the line of stuffed animals on the floor: "I expect you to sit quietly. No purring, peeping, pecking, or trumpeting. That means you," she said to Luciana's elephant.

Ms. Parker picked up a stack of ads on newsprint that she'd gotten from the grocery store. "Today we're going to create some song-and-dance routines related to word problems," she announced. "Everybody okay with that? Let's make this fun. The ads are organized by sections. Check 'em out."

"Want to be my partner?" asked Nancy. "You can sing and I can dance."

"I think I am getting laryngitis," Carson whispered.

"But you didn't have laryngitis during PE!" Nancy said.

"It came on suddenly," said Carson.

"Maybe you yelled too loud when you were Hula-Hooping."

"I did not!" shouted Carson.

"See? There's nothing wrong with your voice, you faker! Hey! There are some great deals in here!" Her eyes lit up. "Let's plan a party for Mr. Lipman's fortieth!"

Nancy got right to business making up a menu and a shopping list. She tallied it up. "Bad news. We're already at $1,286.34. Hmm." She looked at Carson. "Think maybe we should switch from grilled lobster drizzled with melted organic butter to hot dogs with chili on top?"

"Okay, sure."

"Time's up," Ms. Parker sang out. "Who's ready? Nancy? Carson?"

"Not ready," said Nancy. "Plus, we're completely over budget."

"What budget?"

"A surprise-party budget. Mr. Lipman's fortieth is coming up."

"Mr. Lipman is already turning forty?"

"He's thirty-eight. We're getting him used to the idea," said Nancy.

"This math assignment was supposed to involve music and dance," said Ms. Parker. "Not a party plan."

"Well, we haven't gotten to the song-and-dance routine yet. That's going to be Carson's department. Can he borrow a Hula-Hoop? Does Hula-Hooping count as dancing?"

"Yes. Your group's up first on Monday."

Yikes!

Carson watched the other groups perform. They all were bad, but the country song about fried green tomatoes and fresh corn on the cob was the worst one of all.

He was happy to get out of there.

Carson walked with the kids back to Mr. Lipman's room, passing Ms. Parker's Switcheroo students on their way back to their class. He was tired. Hungry, too. Especially after all that talk about sizzling lobster tails.

He wandered into his classroom and sat down.

Mr. Lipman was standing at the front of the classroom, saying nothing. The kids got quieter and quieter when they saw how grumpy he looked.

"It has just this minute been brought to my attention that someone has taken Parks's yo-yo from the June Box. Does anybody know anything about this?"

No one spoke.

Carson knew something about it. He knew quite a bit about it, actually. For starters, it wasn't actually Parks's yo-yo. He also knew it was Chloe's brother Joey's yo-yo, and that it was Zoe's fault Parks got it taken away. But a green yo-yo was the last thing he was concerned about at the moment. He had glanced at his pack.

What was it doing on the floor?

Instead of hanging from the hook where he left it.

"Because," continued Mr. Lipman, "I could not be more clear on this situation. Whoever has removed Parks's yo-yo from the box needs to bring it forward."

He looked from student to student.

Carson stared at his pack. *Maybe someone from Math Switcheroo knocked my pack off the hook accidentally,* he thought.

And left it sitting on the floor.

But this didn't seem like a very good time to ask Mr. Lipman if he could hang it back up. Even though Moose was basically lying facedown, with his nose on the hard, cold, dirty tiles. Technically, Moose just was cloth, thread, and stuffing, but still.

Carson couldn't stand it!

He raised his hand. "Mr. Lipman? Is it okay if I hang my pack back up?"

Mr. Lipman said, "If anyone has any information they want to share with me about the missing yo-yo, please feel free to meet with me individually or even write a note."

"Does it have to be in proper letter format?" asked Zach.

"No. And yes, Carson. You may hang up your pack."

Carson hurried over to his pack and picked it up by the handle.

But he saw in a heartbeat that . . .

Something was wrong!

His pack was empty, and the zipper was . . .

Unzipped!

The zipper was unzipped and Moose . . .

Was gone!

Panicked, he turned to Mr. Lipman. "Somebody took something out of my pack."

"What was taken?"

"A stuffed animal."

"Are you sure? What does it look like?"

Carson had to take a moment to get himself together. No need to go into the missing antlers, wattles, cropped tail, and bald ears. "It's . . . um. It's a small brown mammal."

"Anybody seen a small brown stuffed mammal?"

"Aaaahhhh-chooooooooooooo!" roared Wes.

Carson shot a look over at him. Wes's face was in his desk, and the desk lid was balanced on top of his head.

"Weston? That is ab-so-lute-ly *un*acceptable," said Mr. Lipman.

Wes looked up from over the enormous wad of tissues he was holding against his face. "I'm using tissues but also corralling any and all germ escapees in the interior desk area."

"*Not* a good strategy," said Mr. Lipman.

"Well, I'm going to the doctor after school to see what we can do about the Dandy dander dilemma."

"Fine."

Mr. Lipman turned to Carson. "Start by checking the lost and found. Look carefully and properly."

Carson hurried to the multipurpose room. He looked carefully and properly through the large bin. Moose wouldn't be in the bin!

Still, he looked all the way down, down, down to the bottom, through acorn sweatshirts, squirrel beanies, acorn scarves.

When he got back, kids were coloring pictures of endangered-species habitats. The class was working so quietly you could hear a crayon drop on the rug. And Wes had dropped several crayons on the rug and was under the desks, rounding them up.

Mr. Lipman asked, "No luck?"

"Nope."

Carson sat down.

"It will show up."

Nancy whispered, "Pssst! I have an idea. Why not leave your pack on the hook with a sign on it: RETURN BROWN STUFFED MAMMAL HERE. NO QUESTIONS ASKED."

"Okay."

She helped Carson make the sign with markers.

Chloe and Zoe followed suit. They made a sign that said RETURN GREEN YO-YO HERE. NO QUESTIONS ASKED.

They attached the sign to the June Box with some tape they found in a drawer near the sink.

"Girls? If that yo-yo reappears, I'm going to have a few questions, that's for sure."

The bell rang.

Wes headed for the door, dragging his pack. He looked tired. His eyes were red. "Feel better, Wes!"

"Thanks."

"Hope those allergies clear up!"

"Thanks."

"Ask your grandmother if you can bring a backup box of tissues."

"Okay."

Carson had a brief and, yes, ridiculous mission to accomplish. No one was looking, so he quickly ducked behind the rolling book cart.

A moment later, he heard someone moan:

"Oh.

"My.

"*Gosh!*

"Mr. Lipman? Weston Walker just walked off with my acorn sweatshirt! Did you see how fat his pack was?"

"Calm down, Chloe."

Chloe didn't calm down. She got more upset!

"First Weston bugs me to trade sweatshirts. I say no. And so the guy just takes mine off my hook, shoves it in his pack, and leaves. Right under your nose. That *rat!*"

"Why would he take your sweatshirt? He's twice your size."

"He could squeeze into it!"

Carson peered over the top of the book cart. Wow. Chloe was really losing it.

"I cannot be*lieve* Weston Walker just walks out of here with Carson's stuffed mammal and my acorn sweatshirt stuffed in his pack!"

Mr. Lipman stared at her.

"Bet you anything Parks's green yo-yo is in there, too. What else around here is missing?"

She looked around the room.

"You're more worried about Weston's stuffy nose than the stuff he stuffed in his pack!"

"Chloe? Bus. B-U-S. You're just about to miss it."

As Chloe stamped out, Carson emerged from behind the cart, whistling softly. He waved good-bye to Mr. Lipman.

"I'm sure it'll turn up," Mr. Lipman said gently.

"Right."

20. HELLO,
Heartache

Carson's dad was leaning against the Porsche with his arms folded against his chest, waiting for him. "Where's your pack?" he called.

Carson pointed back at the school. He walked up to his dad and quietly told him about Moose getting stolen and the note he and Nancy made.

"What?! Shall I go in there and talk to your teacher about this?"

"No thanks, Dad. Moose'll show up."

"Where's your sweatshirt?"

Carson pointed at the school again.

Carson couldn't bring himself to tell his dad that,

just as the bell rang, he suddenly thought of the sound of four little hooves clattering around the empty hallways of Valley Oak School as Moose frantically searched for him.

And just for that moment, just that one moment, Moose became as real as he ever had been, back when Carson was a little kid. Back when Dr. Tichenal heard his heartbeat.

Well, maybe it was for more than one moment.

Maybe it was for two moments.

Or three.

Carson knew it wasn't possible, but it did cross his mind that Moose might bed down behind the book cart for a couple of nights.

That's where his hoodie was: folded up in the corner behind the rolling book cart. It was a secret spot. A perfect spot for a moose to hide. You could tell by the crumpled-up candy wrappers, balled-up papers, and checkers on the floor that even the Deputy Dustbusters had never been back there.

He figured that the scent of Carson on Carson's hoodie might comfort Moose.

Carson frowned.

He hoped that the hoodie hadn't been washed and dried and shrunk and washed and dried and shrunk too many times.

If it had, there would be no familiar scent left in it at all.

Grow up! Carson told himself.

Well, he was trying.

"You want to go back for it?" his dad asked.

"Nah. I can wear my jacket."

After supper, Carson watched TV, a program about how to hollow out a tree and make a canoe.

They showed two people in the finished canoe, dipping their paddles into the quiet river. A moose was standing at the edge of the water. It lifted its magnificent rack of antlers and gazed in their direction as they passed by.

With water drizzling from its muzzle.

"I'm thinking that Weston Walker may have Moose," Carson quietly told his father. "Just a hunch."

"Just a hunch?"

"Well . . . maybe more than a hunch."

"How so?"

"A girl named Chloe pointed out that at the same time Moose vanished, a green yo-yo was heisted from the June Box, a green yo-yo that Weston Walker had previously shown an interest in.

"Also, she mentioned that he had been hounding her to trade hoodies with her, and hers mysteriously went missing, just moments before he was seen leaving with an overstuffed backpack."

"Hmmm."

"And we had just had Clean Out That Backpack, Dagnabbit! Day."

"Wow. I don't know what to say about this, son."

"Neither do I, Dad."

Carson crawled into bed.

There was a thump on the door and it swung open. What?!

His dad was holding Mrs. Nibblenose! At arm's length, but nonetheless, he was gently and carefully holding her. Her tail was waving in a scary way. Lashing, kind of.

"Look at this nice lady!" he said.

Good for him! Carson's dad had made it over the hump.

"She says she wants to snuggle with you for a little while."

"Her?"

His dad added, "Not all night, of course, but for a few minutes."

Carson's dad put Mrs. Nibblenose on the pillow, but Mrs. Nibblenose wasn't into snuggling up, just sniffing and wiggling. Sniffing and burrowing under the covers. Soon she was all the way down at Carson's feet. Her whiskers tickled his ankles!

"Thanks anyway, Dad." Carson handed back Mrs. Nibblenose. "That was brave, Dad."

"Thank you, son."

After the Mrs. Nibblenose disturbance, Carson wasn't sleepy.

He turned on the light and worked awhile on his Whiz Quiz poem.

"You awake in there, Dad?"

"Yes!"

"Crack, smack, crash, smash, crunch," Carson called. "Good onomatopoeias?"

"Excellent!"

"Okay. Then here's another clue. Crunches lunches."

"Squirrel?"

"No. But I wish a squirrel would jump out of a tree and land on Weston Walker's shoulder and chatter its teeth in his face."

"Let's not demonize Weston. We have no proof that he's a yo-yo, moose, and hoodie thief."

"But the evidence suggests that, don't you think?"

"Sort of."

His dad showed up at the doorway again, this time with Genevieve. "We can bend the basket rules occasionally."

Genevieve jumped onto the bed, flopped on her back, and waved her tail. She tried to stand on her head for a minute. Then she flipped over, stood up, and stuck her head under the covers and tossed them around. She lay down beside Carson, panting loudly, with her mouth open and her tongue hanging out. After a while, she yawned, closed her mouth, and put her nose on the sheet. And looked at Carson, and rolled her eyes from one side to the other.

She slept with Carson, sprawled on the bed diagonally and trapping the covers underneath her.

Carson woke up and encouraged her to get up and stretch her legs. He got up, too, and looked through the black windowpane. Fog had rolled in and covered the stars, but he knew they were out there somewhere.

Carson had made it halfway through his first soggy, unstarlit, and moonless night without Moose in his life, and actually he felt good about it.

For about one minute at a time.

Yes, it was time to move on from Moose, time to put him away.

Set him up on a shelf.

But first he had to get him back!

It was the principle of it!

Carson was furious.

Maybe he would confront Wes.

He went back to bed.

When Carson woke up in the morning, his dad was reading the newspaper in the kitchen. "Sleep okay?"

"Yup."

"Guess what's going on this weekend? A classic-car and hot-rod show in Penngrove, across the Richmond–San Rafael Bridge and up the highway about forty-five minutes. There's a free rock 'n' roll band, classic cars, food, and a rat-rod contest. Shall we go?"

"What's a rat rod?"

"No clue. Sounds interesting, though!"

They put Genevieve outside in the yard. Genevieve's gigantic water bowl was muddy because she enjoyed dropping her ball in it, then standing with her front legs in it and staring at the ball. Carson dumped it out and refilled it with the hose. She barked at the water when it was coming out of the nozzle. He tossed the tennis ball to the fence, and she brought it to the water bowl. All was good. Carson went out the gate, making triple sure it was latched.

Carson and his dad drove through the neighborhood and down to the highway entrance. They paid the toll. As they started across the bridge, Carson looked down at the water below. A huge black and red tanker, with a tugboat beside it, was docked at a pier.

Across the bay, Claude Monet sailboats were heeling into the wind. Beyond them, on the other side of the water, skyscrapers of San Francisco rose up and disappeared into the clouds.

Carson and his dad drove up the highway, which

was lined with redwood trees. They got to Penngrove and followed signs to Penngrove Park. They parked the Porsche in the gravel lot, far away from the other cars, so they wouldn't get a door ding.

They bought tickets from some guys wearing HOT ROD HOODLUMS hats who said, "Keep the stub for the drawing, dudes."

Carson put his into his shirt pocket, and they wandered in.

The classic cars were parked on the baseball field. So many, it was hard to pick a favorite, but Carson's dad said that, for him, the '34 Packard convertible was right on up there with the '56 Porsche Speedster and the '57 Nomad.

Rat rods were parked in a separate section, with scruffy owners standing around or else leaning against their cars.

The winning rat rod looked like it was shot up out in the desert, left there for ten years, hauled up out of a ravine, then squashed.

A skinny guy with a tattoo of a monarch butterfly on his Adam's apple asked Carson if he wanted to sit in it, and Carson did.

He opened the rusty door and Carson climbed in.

Wow!

The windshield was only about eight inches high!

After that, Carson and his dad had tacos from a lunch truck and listened to the band play some oldies but goodies on a bandstand inside a wooden gazebo. The lead singer looked like Elvis, with black sideburns, black hair slicked back, and a pack of cigarettes rolled up in his T-shirt sleeve.

Right after the band played "Sweet Little Sixteen," they took a break, and a guy went up onto the bandstand to announce the numbers on the winning ticket.

He read them slowly: "9-9-9-7-6-5-2."

The crowd was quiet.

Then he read them again.

"Anybody out there with 9-9-9-7-6-5-2?"

Carson fumbled in his shirt pocket.

It was Carson's number!

He was the winner of a rebuilt transmission for a '32 Ford!

"Come on up!" the guy said into the microphone. And when Carson came up, the guy rested his elbow on Carson's shoulder and pretended to lean on him.

"Now all ya need is to grow up, get yourself a driver's license, get yourself a job, and get the rest of the '32 Ford coupe that goes along with it!"

Everybody clapped and cheered and the band struck up: "Wake up, little Susie! We gotta go home."

Carson's dad accepted an invitation to dance with a woman in a ponytail wearing saddle shoes, white bobby socks, a felt poodle skirt, a pink sweater, and pink lipstick and holding a large paper cup full of root beer.

Some guys helped them load the transmission into the Porsche, and they headed home.

They spent Sunday quietly.

A neighbor came over and helped them get the transmission into the garage. In a few years, Carson would be all grown-up, with his own '32 Ford coupe, maybe with a rumble seat. By then, the last thing on his mind would be having a stuffed moose.

21. HELLO,
Nick

On Monday morning, Carson quietly ate his break-fast: Egg in a Nest. It looked like a big yellow eyeball staring at him.

"If Moose doesn't turn up, so be it. I'm past sleep-ing with a stuffed animal. And, Dad? I don't need a birthday party this year. I don't want a trail ride. Let's just you and me hang out."

"Let's not decide that now."

Carson frowned. "And let's not make a classroom party, either."

His dad said, "I feel like I have a stake in this, too, actually. I share a stake in this because Moose was waiting for you in your crib the day I brought you home." He put his hand on Carson's arm. "Which was the happiest day of my life. Right along with every day I've had with you ever since. I feel sentimental about him. So yes, I'd like to have the goal of getting him back, and then you can put him up on a shelf, or put him away if that's what you want to do."

"I do. What's the cutoff age for sleeping with a stuffed moose, anyway?"

"No set age. There aren't guidelines or rules for everything."

"Does nine seem about right?"

"Maybe."

"That's about halfway to getting a driver's license."

"Okay, nine then, if you say so."

Carson waited by the classroom door till the bell rang and then walked in. The sign was still up; his pack was still empty.

He glanced over at Wes's desk.

He was absent.

How convenient!

Carson wondered if Wes was sitting at home all

zipped up snug in Chloe's sweatshirt, playing with Dandy, Moose, and a green yo-yo.

Dandy better not be biting Moose.

Darn Wes, anyway!

After the flag salute and attendance, a woman wearing workout gear appeared at the door. A Valley Oak backpack was hanging from her shoulder.

"Mr. Lipman?"

"Yes?"

"Melissa Johnson here. My son, Parks, has you for math."

"Right."

"And oh my gosh! He left school straight from your math class on Friday. Remember? He had all his things with him? Well, apparently he grabbed the wrong pack and chucked it into the back of my car with his trumpet and all his other stuff. We took my husband's SUV to Tahoe and were gone all weekend."

Carson looked over at the Valley Oak pack hanging on his hook with the note on it. He looked at the backpack hanging from Parks's mom's shoulder.

His heart thumped.

"There's an adorable stuffed beast in it of some sort. Maybe a snapping turtle or dinosaur. In any case, it looks like it's been loved half to death!" She unzipped the zipper. "Ta-da!" She pulled Moose out. "Anybody know this guy?" She gave him a big squeeze, and a big fat kiss on his back.

"Me," squeaked Carson.

"Me," he said in a regular voice.

She handed Moose to Carson. "Sorry about the mix-up. I really am. But . . . what kind of a critter is this?"

Carson pretended he didn't hear her.

The class was quiet.

Carson balled up the RETURN BROWN STUFFED MAMMAL HERE. NO QUESTIONS ASKED sign, and they switched out the packs.

Parks's mom waved to everybody. "Have a great day, everyone! Buh-bye!"

"Wait!" cried Chloe. "Did Parks accidentally also grab the wrong sweatshirt, by any chance? My hook is right by Carson's."

"I'll ask."

"I really would like to have my sweatshirt back!"

"We'll look."

Chloe's shoulders slumped.

"That sweatshirt's very special to me."

"Okay, yes, I understand. I'll look."

"I really need it!"

"Okay, fine. I'll look."

When Carson's dad pulled up in the Porsche after school, Carson couldn't resist: he stood on the sidewalk, sadly looking down at the cement. His dad asked, "No luck?"

Carson climbed into the car.

"Where do we go from here?" his dad asked him.

Carson said, "I dunno. Just forget about him, I guess."

Carson's dad slowly pulled out of the parking lot. "I'm not sure I agree, Carson."

"It's hard, I know. But you'll just have to deal with it, Dad. You're almost fifty!"

"I'm forty-six years old, Carson."

He shifted from first, to second, to third. Then he slowed and stopped at a red light.

Carson snuck Moose out of his pack and bonked his dad on his neck and ear and said, "Hello, Nick."

When Carson's dad turned his head, he was looking directly into Moose's eyes.

"What the?! Ha! Are you *kidding* me?"

"Nope! He spent the weekend in my pack in the back of Parks's mom's car parked out back in Parks's driveway when they went to Tahoe in his dad's SUV."

"You're not serious!"

"I *am* serious. Parks was in such a hurry to leave school early he accidentally took my pack and left his."

"Well, *duh*. Like a pack rat! Take one, leave one. Between the two of us we didn't think of that," said Carson's dad. "But so it goes. All's well that ends well."

"Boy, Dad. You can say that again!"

"But so it goes. All's well that ends well."

22. GOOD-BYE,
Hair Frog

Carson didn't have quite as much enthusiasm for paragraphs as Mr. Lipman did. In fact, on a scale of one to ten, Carson's enthusiasm for paragraphs was maybe a five, at the most.

But he was still determined to get it right.

Mr. Lipman called out, "Paragraphs! Ready?"

The kids answered all at once, "Eeeee-yeah!"

Mr. Lipman began his paragraph cheer—and the kids joined in:

Topic sentence, topic sentence, sis koom bah!
Examples to support it—rah! rah! rah!
FACT. DETAIL!

FACT. DETAIL!
FACT. DETAIL!
G–o–o–o–o–o–o–o, conclusion!
Rah!

He plopped a red day pack on his desk. "Let's do this!" He walked to the whiteboard and wrote: *When I go on a day hike, I always bring my day pack with me, filled with essential items.*

He turned to the class. "This is the topic sentence."

He rapped on the words. "Stick to it!"

Then he paused. "Once I was in Yosemite Valley. I was lying in my sleeping bag under the stars, on my back, with my day pack for a pillow, snoring. A bear smelled my mouth."

"What did you do?" Wes asked.

"I can't elaborate. We're in the middle of writing a paragraph."

Wes threw up his arms. "Come *on!*"

"Sorry. We have to stick to the topic. What's something important that I would carry in my day pack?" asked Mr. Lipman. "Sydney?"

"A water bottle," she grumbled.

"Fact!" Mr. Lipman wrote: *The first thing I put in my day pack is a water bottle.* He folded his arms on his chest. "Why?"

"So you won't get dehydrated," mumbled Sydney.

"Detail!" Mr. Lipman wrote: *I bring water so I won't get dehydrated.*

Sydney said, "I see no good reason why you can't tell Wes about the bear sniffing your teeth. Other people want to hear it, too!"

Mr. Lipman ignored her. He unzipped one of the outside pack pockets and took out a flimsy, see-through, bucket-shaped army-green object made of lightweight mosquito netting. He pulled it over his head and face and stared at the class through the green gauze.

The kids stared back.

"Shall I include my mosquito mask?"

Nobody answered.

"Do I *always* bring a mosquito mask? No. I don't. Stick to the topic: items I *always* bring. Essentials."

Mr. Lipman pulled the mask off and stuffed it back into the pocket. "Carson?"

Carson jumped.

"You listening?"

"Yes!"

"What else do you think might be in my pack here that you consider important enough to include in the paragraph? Are these?" Mr. Lipman pulled out a box of crayons. "I might like to color on some tree trunks or rocks along the way." He pulled out a roll of masking tape. "This okay?" He pulled out a small travel iron by the cord. "How about this, then?"

Mr. Lipman pulled out a bow tie. He opened his closet door, looked in the mirror, and tied the tie into a perfect bow. He turned around and smiled at the class. "All dressed up and ready to hike to a prom. Right? I'll bring my travel iron in case I need to iron my shirt, and the masking tape to tape up my pants if the cuffs are too long. So I won't step on them."

Oswaldo raised his hand. "At my brother's school, instead of a prom you can go to a morp, which is 'prom' spelled backward."

Mr. Lipman rubbed his nose. "Dusty closet."

"Kids who don't want to get all dressed up and go to the senior prom have the choice of going to the senior morp instead."

"Ah . . ."

"They wear flannel pj's and bring stuffed animals."

"Ah . . ."

"And eat pizza . . ."

"Ah . . ."

"And stay up all night watching scary movies."

"Ah-*pooch*!" Mr. Lipman sneezed into a wad of tissues, dropped them into the trash, and then helped himself to a squirt of hand sanitizer. "Nancy? Please say thanks again to your mom for the Germbegone pump bottle."

"I will. Mr. Lipman?"

"Yes?"

"Is 'ah-*pooch*' an onomatopoeia?"

"Negative."

"Can we have a morp like at Oswaldo's brother's school?" asked Sydney.

"No. No morp, Sydney. If it rains on the campout, as I have explained, I have rented six six-person, free-standing tents with special tarps that go underneath— and rain flies."

"In other words," said Wes, "everybody will have to suck it up."

"Exactly," said Mr. Lipman.

"But what if it pours? What if it soaks the ground?" asked Sydney. "Then can we have the morp? What if it's raining cats and dogs and the Green Gulch group campground turns into a huge mucky mud puddle?"

"If it rains cats and dogs, I suppose we'll have a soggy grouchy group of woofing and meowing mucky wet muddy mammals to deal with," Mr. Lipman said.

Nancy took out her onomatopoeia list and added "woof" and "meow."

"What if the stream in the meadow swells up and floods our tents!" said Sydney.

"Stop saying that!" cried Shelly. "You'll make it happen!"

"No she won't," said Mr. Lipman. "You can't make it rain a week from now by talking about it. But since you're what-iffing—as you know, we have a phone tree. We'll call off the campout."

The class moaned.

"Call off the campout? Completely? Why?!" cried Sydney. "We can morph it into a morp! The parents can bring Weber grills and set 'em up in the patio area right here at the school. Or we can eat pizza in the multipurpose room. Like the kids in Oswaldo's big brother's school."

"Yeah!" cried some other kids.

"Fine. Fine. Fine. If we get rained out, we'll have ourselves a morp. Onward! What else is in my pack?"

"But wait a minute. What about s'mores?" said Sydney. "We'll have to skip s'mores if we have a morp." She sadly added, "No campfire. No singing around the campfire. What a bummer."

"Sydney? We'll have morp s'mores," said Mr. Lipman. "Cold morp marshmallows, chilly chocolate bars, and snappy graham crackers. Sound good?"

"No."

"Well, too bad. The Complaint Department is closed."

"Are there black bears in Green Gulch?" asked Oswaldo.

"No."

"Snakes?" asked Oswaldo.

"No. Not poisonous ones, anyway."

"Cougars?"

"No."

"Bobcats?"

"Bears! Bobcats! Cougars! All mammals. Snakes—are not. Because?" He looked at Sydney.

"They're not hairy."

Carson heard a rattly sound. Wes was creeping toward Mr. Lipman, rattling a small see-through plastic box of Fresh Breath Refresherettes in one hand and holding his other hand with two fingers sticking up and curled a little bit, like fangs.

He suddenly struck them into the back of his hand.

"I got bit!"

He slid onto the floor and writhed around, squeezing his wrist. "I got bit! I got bit!"

"Get up, Wes. Fresh Breath Refresherettes are the same as candies! Fork 'em over."

Wes sat up and tossed the box to Mr. Lipman.

"Adios till June," said Mr. Lipman as he dropped them into the June Box. "In you go with the Teenie Weenie Jelly Beanies."

"What did you do when the bear smelled your tongue?!" cried Sydney.

"Calm down. Please! I closed my mouth. And I

promised myself I would never eat pan-fried trout again. And I vowed never to use for a pillow a pack that had gorp in it."

"Which is what?" asked Sydney.

"Which is a healthy mix of nuts, raisins, et cetera. We'll eat gorp at the morp. Okay? Now. Despite my excellent props, I must admit this paragraph lesson has been a complete bust."

He put the iron, bow tie, and masking tape back into his pack. "Let's move on to Twenty Questions."

"You should have eaten a few Bad-Breath Bullets before you went to sleep," Wes told him.

"I thought you said they were pellets."

"The bigger ones are bullets. The biggest ones are Bad Breath Bombs."

"Well, bears may be attracted to Bad-Breath Bombs, too. They're attracted to all kinds of smelly stuff: toothpaste, shaving cream, deodorant, et cetera. Anyway, onward to Twenty Questions."

Weston asked, "Am I kicked out of the morp or just out of the camping trip?"

Mr. Lipman pinched his upper lip. "Camping trip, yes. Morp, no. But your grandmother has to come with you. And spend the entire night. Tell her I said so."

"Can she bring the ingredients for make-it-yourself pizza? To bake in the oven in the multipurpose room? And put little sliced circles of hot dogs on top?"

"Whatever you say, Wes. Twenty Questions, let's go. Who's up?"

Mr. Lipman reached into the Star Jar.

"Okay, who's first this time? . . . Num-ber . . ."

"Watch, it won't be me. And it better not be fourteen," grumbled Sydney.

Mr. Lipman read the number. ". . . eighteen? Who's eighteen?"

"Meeeeee!" Shelly squealed. "I knew you would pick me! I thought positively and it happened." She ran to the whiteboard and uncapped an erasable marker. "I visualized this moment and it worked!"

Mr. Lipman turned to Sydney. "The power of thinking positively," he told her. "Try it sometime!"

"I am. I'm closing my eyes and thinking that tongue depressors with numbers on them are positively depressing," Sydney told him.

"Can we start?" said Shelly.

"Wait! Wait! Wait! I forgot my cap," Mr. Lipman told her. He put on his detective's cap. He yanked down the brims. Front, then back. "Okay, ready."

Luciana raised her hand. "Can it run fast?"

"Very."

Shelly drew a small vertical line on the board.

"Is it a rabbit?"

"No." She drew another line next to the first one.

"Does it have fuzzy ears?" asked Eva.

"Yes."

Shelly drew another line.

Zach asked, "Is it fuzzy all over?"

Shelly said, "It's hairy all over."

"A hair frog!" yelled Wes.

Shelly drew two more lines. Sydney frowned at him. "There's no such thing as a hair frog."

"Yes there is! There was a huge, hairy hair frog hopping in my house behind a hamper. My grandma released it back into the wild—into the birdbath. Its hair fell off in the water."

"Once upon a time in Whoppersville there lived a hair frog . . . ," began Cody. "And a beautiful princess sat by the birdbath and kissed it, and it turned into an ape prince."

"Cody? Be appropriate. Let's move on," said Mr. Lipman. Carson heard him whisper "Heaven help me" under his breath.

Zach asked, "Does it snort?"

"A little bit."

She drew a line.

"Is it a bull?"

"No." She drew a line.

"Kids?" interrupted Mr. Lipman. "Strategy. Twenty Questions is a thinking game, not a guessing game. Begin with general questions, then move to specific questions. Like: Does it have pointy teeth or flat teeth? Or: Does it have hooves or pads on its feet?"

"Is it Mrs. Nibblenose?" asked somebody.

Shelly drew a line and shook her head. "Rats don't snort."

"Wait a minute," said Mr. Lipman. "Are any of you listening to me? You're running out of questions, fast. Before you ask a specific animal, ask general questions, like: Herbivore or carnivore? Does it eat grass? Or other animals? Does it have antlers, or a horn?"

Shelly drew six more lines. Mr. Lipman tried to defend himself. "I was making suggestions. Not asking questions."

"They *were* questions," said Shelly. "Several in a row, and you're only supposed to ask *one*. One at a time, please."

"Referee?" Mr. Lipman said.

Matthew thought a minute. "They were questions," he decided. "Your voice went up at the end."

"Okay, next time I'll keep my mouth shut," said Mr. Lipman.

"But Shelly didn't answer any of the questions!" moaned Sydney. "And she put up six points against us!"

"It has a horn," said Shelly.

"It's a Dodge Ram truck!" yelled Wes.

"I quit," said Sydney.

Shelly drew another line.

Nancy raised her hand. "Does it love lots of lovely little leaves?"

"Certain ones."

"*Caterpillar!*" Wes called out.

Mr. Lipman took off his cap and threw it on his desk.

"Is it bigger than a flea?" asked Zoe.

"Yes."

"Is it smaller than a horse?" asked Chloe.

"Not really."

"Is it a pony?" asked Matthew.

"Nope."

"Flat feet or pointy feet?"

"Flat."

"Is it Carson's little lost brown mammal?" Cody asked. A little smile crept across his face.

Wes turned to him. "How about you shut your trap."

Mr. Lipman borrowed the marker from Shelly and wrote *Weston Walker* on the board.

"Please continue," he told the class.

"Can it fly?" asked Nancy.

"Yes."

"A mammal can*not* fly!" said Sydney.

"I thought you quit," said Shelly.

"A bat is a mammal. And a bat can fly . . . ," said Zach.

Shelly's eyes were twinkling. "He's right. A bat can fly. You guys have one more question. Go on: ask it."

"Okay," said Sydney. She paused.

"Don't ask it!" cried Cody. "Bats don't have flat feet. I don't think bats even have feet!"

"Yes they do!"

"All righty, then," said Sydney. "I'll ask it: Is it a bat?"

"No. It is *not* a bat. Your twenty questions are up. I won."

Shelly took the cap off the bottom of the marker, replaced it over the top, and clicked it closed.

She skipped back to her seat.

She sat down and Nancy looked over at her. "It was a unicorn, wasn't it?"

"Yip."

Mr. Lipman reluctantly gave Shelly a Bonus Buck.

After school, the first question Carson asked when he got into the car was: "Have you ever heard of a hair frog, Dad?"

"A hair frog? No, I can't say as I have."

"Wes said there was one hopping behind his hamper. What do you think about that?"

His dad turned off the radio. "What I think about that is that a hair frog may well be related to a dust bunny. And somebody in Wes's house needs to get with a vacuum."

"Well, he said hair fell off the frog in the birdbath. Then it was bald."

"I rest my case."

"Wow. I can never figure out whether Wes is telling the truth or making stuff up," sighed Carson.

"Well, maybe you will as you get to know him better. Maybe at the campout."

"He's not allowed to come because he poses a supervision problem."

"Ah."

23. HELLO,
Morp!

The night before the campout, Carson woke up to the sound of wind swirling in the trees and rain splattering against his window. He got out of bed and looked into the darkness. It was black outside, except for the streetlamp that marked the end of his driveway. Rain was steadily falling through the light. He climbed back into bed.

Soon he was fast asleep.

In a dream he was chased by a huge furry frog. It had big clumps of hair growing out of its back. Carson was running as fast as he could, but he kept hearing the flap-flapping of the frog's enormous flat webbed feet coming closer and closer up behind him. He jumped into a stream and the huge frog flopped in after him, and when it came up from the bottom of the stream, it was a gigantic bald gorilla. Birds were circling around its head, and it was snapping at them with slimy, pointed yellow teeth. Carson tried to get away, but it grabbed his ankle and pulled him under the water.

Carson awoke to the sound of the phone ringing. Yay! It was just a dream. He heard his dad say, "Nick Blum here." Then a pause. "Yeah, that's what we figured. Yup. Came down in buckets all night long. Okay then, five o'clock in the multipurpose room."

As it turned out, the morp was fine—in fact, fun.

Carson was happy that Wes was allowed to come, especially because he brought his grandma.

The Stink Eye came in handy, too. Wes's grandma had the ability to raise just one eyebrow in his direction and at the same time lower the other eyebrow, which was effective.

Scary, actually!

She did bring the hot dogs and make-your-own-pizza ingredients. The oven in the multipurpose kitchen didn't work. But Chloe and Zoe discovered a big toaster oven way, way in the back of the cupboard marked PTA.

Wes's grandma dragged it out, dusted it off, and plugged it in. Then she rolled out the pizza dough, cut it into strips, and wrapped the hot dogs up in the strips, with just the tips of the hot dogs sticking out.

They were kind of like pigs in a blanket, but gorier!

She baked them in the toaster oven till the dough was crispy and the dogs were steamy hot. She took them out and dunked one end of each wrapped hot dog in pizza sauce. And served them on a big aluminum tray.

They looked like old cutoff mummy fingers, wrapped up in bloody gauze.

Wow!

They were delicious!

Carson's dad, Oswaldo's dad, and Luciana's dad barbecued outside in the rain in the breezeway. Nancy's mom stood by to check the interior temperature of the meat with a thermometer. Abby and Lee

Crabbly stopped by and listened intently to the tri-tip tips.

Quite a bit of sampling went on.

After dinner, everybody played board games. Then Carson's dad, Wes's grandma, and Mr. Lipman figured out how to make s'mores in the toaster oven. Later they plugged it into a thick black extension cord and put it on the floor in the middle of the multipurpose room.

Everybody sat in a big, wide semicircle around it, with the lights off.

They all stared at the pretty orange toaster coils, all lit up, listening to the rain drumming on the rooftop.

They sang a few songs, including "La Bamba."

There was impromptu entertainment: Zach juggled hats, Shelly did an interpretive dance with scarves, Sydney recited part of a depressing and creepy poem about a raven.

Chloe and Zoe showed Mr. Lipman some Halloween decorations they found in a closet, including a huge, sparkling orange harvest moon.

Mr. Lipman taped it to the wall. He had forgotten

to clean out his day pack after the paragraph lesson, so in addition to the roll of masking tape, he also still had a big box of crayons, his bow tie, and his mosquito-netting face mask, which he put on—and told a scary story.

And laughed like this: "*Whoooohahahah hahah ha ha ha ha!*"

And the kids all screamed.

And the thunder rolled.

Nancy brought Ethel and boldly sat with the stuffed otter on her lap. When she was little, she had scribbled under Ethel's nose with a wide-tipped red marker; she was trying to draw lipstick and overshot the mark.

It looked okay.

Sitting on the multipurpose room floor on blankets next to Nancy and Ethel was okay. It wasn't anywhere near as good as sitting around a campfire on the ground.

On the other hand, it was better than sitting in a soggy tent in the rain in a mud puddle in a campground with a fire ring filled with water and floating charcoal. With mammals peering through the soggy trees.

Carson didn't have thick all-wool hiking socks like Patrick's. But having a secret furry four-legged footwarming snoozing Moose at the bottom of his sleeping bag worked out just as well.

In the morning after breakfast, with Chloe and Zoe's help, Liliana's mom located a huge old roll of waxed paper in a drawer that had been stuck shut for a hundred and ten years and hosted an arts-and-crafts project: stained glass windows—grating crayons on a cheese grater and ironing them between sheets of waxed paper with Mr. Lipman's travel iron.

It would have been more fun for Carson if he had been able to report to Gavin and Case about an actual camping trip.

On Sunday afternoon, Carson and his dad returned home from the morp, and thunder began to roll again.

That called for another cup of hot chocolate on the front porch, with Genevieve safely attached to the end of her leash. Carson had a thought: *Would thunder scare a doe and her pups?* He told Genevieve, "Be right back."

He patted the top of her head and set his mug on

the small end table. He hurried inside into the guest room.

Carson's dad had remodeled the cage so that the second Dan Post cowboy boot was now incorporated into the architecture: it was poking out of the side of the cage and functioning as a spare room, nursery, or den.

Carson peered into the boot.

All the pups were sacked out together, cozy and warm.

Mrs. Nibblenose was having a drink from the water bottle—a moment to herself. When thunder rolled again, she moved to the ceramic food dish and sat on the edge, eating a grape.

Life was good.

Carson went back outside.

"Thank you for sacrificing both boots for the privacy and comfort of the rat pups and Mama," Carson quietly said. "Think you'll ever be able to wear those boots again, Dad?"

"Those? Heck yeah I can! Those boots were designed for a hard-ridin' wrangler who sleeps on the ground, eats grub from a chuck wagon, lives out of a saddlebag—who wears the same dusty duds for days on end. When he beds down under the stars, prairie dogs and lizards climb in and out of those boots."

"Will you, Dad?"

"Maybe. I'll go over them with some sanitizing wipes. All ready with your Whiz Quiz poem?"

"I am. Any final thoughts, Dad?"

"Hit me with one more clue."

"Okay. One more clue. Sleeps in a weed bed with its head covered as sparsely as parsley."

"I know, a shrew."

"Nope."

24. HELLO,
Yo-Yo!

Right after Sustained Silent Reading and right before Shape It Up to Shipshape, it would be Carson's turn to try to trick the class with his Whiz Quiz poem, and then Nancy's turn to sing her onomatopoeias.

Carson wandered about the classroom, picking up scraps of paper, straightening books on the shelves. He was aware that his hoodie was still behind the rolling book cart.

So embarrassing!

He was glad nobody knew it was there, not even his dad. He'd been wearing his jacket. But he should definitely retrieve his hoodie soon.

In fact, since no one seemed to be looking in his direction, he should definitely retrieve it immediately.

It was so dusty behind the rolling book cart when Carson squeezed behind it that he wouldn't have been surprised to see a hair frog hop out. He found his hoodie just as he'd left it, except it had a Jolly Rancher candy stuck to the back. When the coast was clear, he came out from behind the cart, put the hoodie on, and wore it, with his wrists poking out of the sleeves.

It was very snug. But Carson liked that. He would feel more confident standing in front of the class with his Whiz Quiz poem if he was zipped up nice and tight. Besides, he had spilled pomegranate juice on the front of his uniform shirt at lunch.

Mr. Lipman settled his detective's cap properly on his head. "Okay, Carson, let's hear it," he said. The class was quiet because Wes was absent.

Carson unfolded his poem. "Face round as a balloon. Nose black as a prune."

"A fat-faced baby lamb," whispered someone.

"Shh!" said Mr. Lipman. "Wait till the end, then raise your hand."

Carson continued: "Sleeps in a weed bed with its

head covered as sparsely as parsley. Can't get sunk. Won't soak. Likes to dunk. Can't croak. Like a froggy, won't get soggy."

Mr. Lipman said, "Hmmmmm. Go on, Carson."

"Braves caves. Air in its hair. Cracks and smacks and bashes and crashes and smashes and crunches its lunches." He paused. "Has a floaty goatee."

He paused.

"Not a lumpy seal. Not a grumpy shabby gabby gull. Not a pouchy grouchy cranky crabby pelican with a limp shrimp in its beak. It's sleek. Bobs for lobster. Gallops with scallops. Floats in its coat like a boat in the water."

Nancy raised her hand. She and Carson locked eyes. "It's an Ethel, isn't it?" she quietly said.

Carson nodded.

Mr. Lipman frowned. "What's an Ethel?"

Nancy answered, "A sea otter!"

"Ah."

Mr. Lipman counted out ten Bonus Bucks and gave them to Carson. "Good job!"

"Thanks."

"So, Nancy? I guess you're up next."

Nancy walked to the front of the class. "Ready, everyone?"

She cleared her throat. She unfolded her paper and looked sideways at Mr. Lipman. And to the tune of "Twinkle, Twinkle, Little Star," she sang:

Achoo
ahem
baa
bah
bam,
bang and
bark and
bash and
bawl.
Beep and
boing and
boink and
bong,
bonk and
boo and
boom and
bump.

Buzz and
cheep and
chirp and
clang,
clank
clap
clatter
click
clink
cluck.

Clunk and
cuckoo
crunch and
ding,
drip and
eek and
fizz and
flick.
Flutter
giggle
growl and
gurgle,

**hiccup
hiss and
honk and
hum.
Itch and
jangle
knock
meow,
moo and
mumble
murmur
neigh.**

Nancy took a deep breath and continued:

**Oink and
ouch and
ow and
phew,
plop and
plunk and
poof and
pop.**

Purr and
quack and
rattle
roar,
rumble
rustle
screech and
shush.
Sizzle
slap and
slurp and
smack,
sneeze and
snip and
snort and
splash.

Squelch and
squish and
swoosh and
thump,
ticktock
tinkle

twang and
tweet.
Vroom and
whack and
wham and
whizz,
whoop and
whoosh and
woof and
yikes.
Zap and
zing and
zip and zoom,

and

that's

it,

folks,

I'm

out

of

room.

Nancy bowed.

"Bravo!" said Mr. Lipman.

The class golf-clapped. Mr. Lipman declared twenty minutes of Ketchup Time—time to catch up on unfinished business.

Nancy collected her Bonus Bucks, and she and Carson signed them and headed out the door.

On the way to the office, Carson jammed his hands into his hoodie pouch.

What the?!

He pulled out the green yo-yo. "What's this doing in my pocket?"

Nancy stepped back and looked at Carson from stem to stern.

"That's *your* hoodie? Turn around."

Carson turned around.

"Looks pretty small to me, Carson."

Carson explained, "My dad shrank it in the dryer."

"Three sizes? Put your arms down at your sides."

"Well, I also think my arms have grown."

"Three inches? Take it off."

Nancy helped Carson pull his arms out of the sleeves. "Aha. What did I tell you?"

She showed Carson the tag. Size S. *Chloe D.* was neatly written in fine-point permanent marker.

Carson quietly said, "Guess it's not mine after all."

Oops.

In his panic about Moose, he must have accidentally grabbed Chloe's sweatshirt off the hook. How the yo-yo got into the pouch, well, that was anybody's guess.

They went into the office and deposited their Bonus Bucks in the Bonus Bucks Box. "Has the Wheel of Fortune been repaired?" Nancy politely asked Mrs. Sweetow.

Mrs. Sweetow pursed her lips and shook her head. "Bad subject."

"Sorry."

"The damage was more extensive than we originally thought." She rolled her eyes. "In fact, it has to be completely reconstructed."

"Wow. That's unfortunate!" said Nancy.

"You can say that again," said Mrs. Sweetow.

Carson didn't say "Wow. That's unfortunate!" again because Mrs. Sweetow was one sour lady about the Wes and the Wheel of Fortune incident.

On the way out the door, Nancy frowned. "What a stinker! Chloe took Parks's yo-yo from the June Box."

"I'm not supposed to tell," said Carson. "But actually, it's Chloe's brother Joey's yo-yo. So I'm not sure what's going on. Are you?"

Nancy closed her eyes and shook her head.

"But I did hear Chloe try to convince Mr. Lipman that Wes put it in his pack. Even I believed Wes had it!"

They slowly walked down the hall.

"Poor Wes," said Nancy. "He gets blamed for everything."

"Well," said Carson. "Sometimes he deserves it. Remember how he broke the wheel? Whose fault was that?"

Nancy whispered, "It may have been improperly

installed." She glanced back over her shoulder. "It's not like Mrs. Sweetow is a professional carpenter or anything."

"What about when Wes forged the numbers on the tongue depressors? Whose fault was that?" asked Carson.

"Actually, I'm not so sure he's the one who did that."

"Well, who else would have done it?"

"Now ya got me. But I do know this much." Nancy picked up Carson's hand. "On his homework papers, Wes makes big, fat, wide, messy numbers. Like this."

Nancy scrawled a big, fat, wide, messy 4 on Carson's palm. "*On* the other hand"—she picked up Carson's other hand—"the numbers on the tongue depressors were neatly drawn. Like this." She neatly and carefully drew a small 4 on Carson's other palm.

It tickled.

"Well, he boosted a foroon out of the cupboard," said Carson. "That much we do know. He ate half my half a burrito with it!"

"Do you know that for a fact?"

"Yes, and he grabbed my mango juice to wash it down."

"Wait. What I'm asking is: Do you know for a fact that he is the one that took the foroon?"

"Pretty much." He glanced at Nancy. "Unless you believe in fairies."

"I have a hunch the Dustbusters may somehow have something to do with this," Nancy said mysteriously. "I'm feeling a bit Nancy Drewish at the moment. And I'd like to see if I'm right about it. You with me?"

"Yup."

25. GOOD-BYE,
Deputy Dustbusters

Ketchup Time was still going on when Carson and Nancy walked in, with some unfinished business. The sweatshirt was casually slung around Nancy's shoulders. They strolled up to Zoe and Chloe.

"There's an ant on your head," Nancy told Zoe.

"Where?"

"It fell off."

Nancy leaned against the counter. "I'm wondering if you two individuals were responsible for forging numbers on Star Jar sticks."

"Us?"

"Yes, you."

"So what if we were."

What would Nancy Drew say to that?

"We love Wes's whoppers," said Zoe. "Wes is a very creative and inventive Whopper Weaver, in case you haven't noticed. The *4* after the *1* and a *1* in front of the *4* was an act of generosity."

"We were upping Wes's chances of getting called on," said Chloe. "And so what?"

Nancy couldn't think of what Nancy Drew would say to that, either.

"We have the right to delegate our Star Jar chances to anybody we want! Those were our numbers and we were sharing them. Star Jar sharing is a life skill."

"But Weston got blamed for it."

"He was happy he got blamed. Wes loves eating lunch with Mr. Lipman. It's Guy Time."

"Did you two happen to have anything to do with the foroon that appeared in Weston's back pocket just before Guy Time?" Carson asked.

Zoe and Chloe made a face at each other. "What's a *foroon?*"

"You know exactly what he's talking about," said Nancy. "A foroon is a plastic eating utensil with little fangs on the edge."

"That's a spork, and yeah, we took one and gave it to Wes, and so what again," Chloe told Nancy. "We heard Wes say he wished he could share Carson's burrito, and we granted his wish! We're the Sporks Fairies!"

Zoe walked up and leaned very, very close to Nancy and said, "So . . . *ha!*"

Nancy sniffed the air. "Hmmmm," she said. "Peppermint breath." She smiled wryly at Carson. "Have the Spork Fairies been helping themselves to the Teenie Weenie Jelly Beanies and the Fresh Breath Refresherettes jailed in the June Box?"

"These items attract Nuisance Ants," Chloe declared.

Nancy and Carson looked at each other. "What's a *Nuisance Ant?*" Nancy asked him, and he shrugged.

"It's a pest ant," Zoe explained. "An ant that comes in from the wild and wreaks havoc in the June Box.

"It's not an easy job, being ant wranglers," Zoe continued. "But we have come to realize that even teensy ants are wildlife."

"Wow. Now I've heard everything," said Nancy.

"I guess you could think of us as Wild Ant

Rescuers," Zoe added. "Similar to Ms. Tapp, but without the blue jackets."

"Unfortunately, mints sometimes fall out of the containers into our hands when we release ants from the containers into the wild. Of course, we're forced to eat the mints because we're supposed to eat the mints we touch. That's the guideline."

Nancy made a face. "Really? Okay. Now I understand. Anyway . . . I'm wondering about something else. . . ."

She took the sweatshirt from her shoulder and stuck the tag under Chloe's nose. "*Chloe D.* Is that you?"

Chloe reached for the sweatshirt but Nancy stepped back. "Not so fast. There seems to be something way, way down in the pocket." She closed one eye and peered into the pouch. "Were the ant wranglers also planning to release a green yo-yo into the wild?"

"Where did you find my sweatshirt?" said Chloe. "I left it on my hook last Friday. The next thing I know, you two walk in with it. Where was it? And you've been rifling through the pockets." She tapped her foot. "Where did you get it from?"

Nancy was quiet. She looked over at Carson.

Carson admitted, "I took it."

"You *did?*"

"Yes, I took it, and I hid it behind the book cart."

Mr. Lipman strolled over. The girls began struggling with the hoodie. There was a brief tug-of-war, with Nancy pulling on one sleeve and Chloe holding the other. "What's going on?"

Zoe reported: "Carson took Chloe's sweatshirt and hid it behind the book cart!"

Mr. Lipman took Carson aside and quietly asked, "Did you?"

"Well . . ."

How would Carson explain this?

"Yes, I did."

Mr. Lipman became very serious. "What's going on?"

Carson shrugged.

"Why would you do something like that?"

Carson was forced to spill the beans. He quietly told Mr. Lipman that he did take Chloe's hoodie and he did hide it in the corner behind the book cart, but it wasn't on purpose. "I must have grabbed her sweatshirt off the hook thinking it was mine. Or maybe hers was hung on my hook. I'm not sure."

Mr. Lipman said nothing.

"The hooks are right next to each other. I thought I was hiding my own hoodie, and I now don't know where mine is."

"But why would you hide your own hoodie behind a book cart, Carson? I don't understand. Why would you hide anybody's hoodie behind a book cart?"

Darn! Carson knew he would ask that question! "Well. I know it's ridiculous to believe a lost stuffed mammal might bed down on it, but—"

Mr. Lipman said, "You don't have to say any more. I get it. And you know what I suspect?"

"What?"

"I suspect your hoodie is in the bottom of the lost-and-found bin. More stuff gets lost in that bin and less stuff gets found there than anyplace else in the school. Go and look right now. Nancy? Please go with Carson. Immediately."

He announced to the class: "This is a simple case of mistaken hoodie identity. There will be no further discussion. Everyone return to your seats. I don't want to hear one more word about this."

Chloe snatched her sweatshirt from Nancy.

Carson and Nancy prowled through the lost and found.

Yup, Carson's hoodie was there, all right. He must have dropped it out in the yard or left it outside the classroom door.

And so was Nancy's baseball mitt from last year!

She socked it a few times to get it back into shape. "Want to come over to my house and play catch sometime?"

"Sure."

"When should we talk to Mr. Lipman about the yo-yo?" Carson asked.

Mr. Lipman was staring into the June Box when Carson and Nancy walked in. "Parks's yo-yo has mysteriously reappeared!" he said.

Zoe exclaimed, "Magic. It's magic!"

And Chloe said, "The fairies returned it!"

"No they didn't and it isn't Parks's yo-yo and you know it," Nancy said.

"And Weston Walker didn't take it, either," Carson added. "And you know that, too!" He looked at Mr. Lipman. "It was in Chloe's sweatshirt pocket."

He turned to the class. "I accidentally took Chloe's sweatshirt to make a bed behind the book cart for my lost moose. And so what." He sat down.

After sorting things out, Mr. Lipman erased Chloe's and Zoe's names from the Deputy List and wrote: *Applications for the Deputy Dustbuster position now being accepted.*

Wow. Maybe Wes could apply!

What a day.

And the hat incident really capped it off.

As Zoe and Chloe were sitting in the Blue Box at afternoon recess, Bob swooped down and grabbed the green pom-pom on Chloe's beanie with his foot and yanked the beanie off her head and flew away with it.

26. HELLO,
Happy Birthday!

Carson's dad rumbled up in the Porsche, on time as always.

"Bad news for Bob!" Carson announced as he opened the door.

"How so?"

"He snatched a hat and dropped it on the library roof."

"Good grief, what an aggressive bird!"

"You can say that again."

"Good grief, what an aggressive bird!"

"And even though Ms. Pierson conceded that the pom-pom may have looked like a pile of pesto from a crow's perspective, it was unacceptable. When a crow makes physical contact with a person or their clothing, that's where she draws the line, because birds are germy."

"Ah."

"So now Patrick and Ella are going to relocate Bob to Green Gulch Park, near the duck pond."

"Ah."

"Maybe you and I can go again for the release! And maybe can we buy Bob some Cheerios? I don't think he can compete with the other crows, Dad. His tail feathers are damaged, and he's lost a leg. They're a bunch of bullies over there."

"Yes, they are."

"Think we could find another plastic great horned owl decoy with yellow glass eyeballs to sit beside him? He loves sitting by Ms. Pierson's owl decoy in the oak tree at school. She's his girlfriend! He's gaga over her."

"He is?"

"Yes! And that is how Patrick's mom is going to catch him—lure him down with the decoy and then cover him with a net. Isn't that a mean trick?"

"Kind of."

"An old crow with a bent beak and broken feathers and a plastic owl. An odd couple. But he loves her, Dad. He never leaves her side."

"You never mentioned he had a chipped beak." He paused. "How badly chipped?"

Carson shrugged. "The kindergarten garden needs the owl back. It was a short-term loan."

"Well, okay then. One beady-eyed owl decoy coming right up for the guy with the chipped beak. Where do we get such a thing?"

"Maybe at Shop Rite in the garden department."

"Fine."

"Dad?"

"What, son?"

"Wes was absent again today. I keep thinking that if he doesn't get better, Dollie might have to find another home for Dandy."

"It doesn't work that way. If Dollie and Wes are unable to provide an adoptive home for Dandy, then they have to return him to the shelter, and the shelter places Dandy in another adoptive home according to their own strict guidelines for dog adoption."

"Oh."

Carson was quiet.

"Well, if they do have to give Dandy up, that would be sad, wouldn't it?"

"Yes, it would. Very sad and very hard."

But Wes was tough—cut from the right stuff.

Whatever happened, Wes could suck it up. But that didn't mean he wouldn't have a broken heart underneath it all.

Good thing Carson and his dad were number one on the shelter's backup list. Actually, they were probably number one and only on the shelter's backup list. Not that Dandy wasn't adorable in his own way.

Carson hoped more than anything that Wes could overcome the allergy problem and keep Dandy. But if worst came to worst, Carson and his dad would step in.

Wes could visit with Dandy at Carson's house, out on the porch with Genevieve, out in the fresh air.

Dandy would be a good play pal for Genevieve. Dandy might not like her at first, because she wasn't a Chihuahua, but any dog who really got to know Genevieve would end up loving her.

And maybe when Wes came to visit Dandy,

Carson could help him get over the rodent issue. He could introduce Wes to Bo.

Then maybe Wes would want to adopt one of Bo's brothers or sisters.

If he did, he could bring his rat pup, and the rat pup and Bo could have a rat-pup playdate while Dandy and Genevieve romped on the lawn.

They sat down on the porch. "Thanks again for helping sponsor the Free-Range Roaming Rat Arena, Dad. And thanks for everything else. Thanks for your help during the morp, for volunteering to come to Career Day, and for volunteering to make pinch pots. Is that how you made my lopsided pencil jar? By pinching it?"

"Yes, it is. . . . I prefer to characterize it as asymmetrical and artful rather than lopsided, but yes."

"Okay, good. Can we pinch other things besides artfully asymmetrical pencil holders?"

"Yes."

"Good. Thanks, Dad. Don't be surprised if Wes yells 'Ouch!' at the top of his lungs every time he pinches the clay."

"I won't."

"Wes is a good guy. He's just a loudmouth, that's all."

"I had an uncle Jim who was as big a loudmouth and as big a ham as Wes is. Uncle Jim was a great guy, too. I wish you could have met him."

Carson's dad grew quiet.

"Me too, Dad."

Carson really did wish he had met Uncle Jim.

He didn't have very many relatives.

Not that he knew of, anyway.

Carson's family tree had only one branch.

He had another whole entire family tree he hadn't seen yet, but that could wait.

Being adopted wasn't that big of a deal for Carson. He already knew that if he wanted to, he and his dad could find out more about his birth parents, and they might look into that sometime down the road. But at least for now, the family he had was perfect.

He had two very grand grandparents.

And he had one wonderful dad.

And even if he met his birth parents, Carson would always have only one dad, one actual dad: the dad sitting beside him in a T-shirt, jeans, and tennis shoes, with his hair poking up on top of his head and a Labrador retriever sitting on his lap, panting in his face.

The best dad in the world.

"Dad?"

"What, son?"

"Let's invite Wes on the birthday ride."

"*Wes*? Are you serious?"

"I am. Wes and Dollie."

"Will he behave himself?"

"No. But Dollie can give him the Stink Eye."

"As he gallops away into a gulch? Why not Patrick and his mother?"

"Blackberry brambles and bees. Remember?"

"Right. Well, what about Nancy and her mom?"

"Would Nancy's mom be willing to accompany Nancy on a sweaty horse that had clumps of muddy sod in its hooves, ate dusty hay, and had slime between its nostrils? A big, smelly beast that whisked flies away with its tail?"

"Why wouldn't she?"

"She's a surgeon!"

"So what. The trail doesn't go through an operating room."

"I know. But still. Wes already knows how to ride."

"He does?"

"I think he'll be a responsible horseback rider on the trail. He's planning to be a rodeo clown. Plus, he rides horseback in the summertime at his aunt Boo and uncle Hunk's quarter-horse farm in Cleveland."

"A quarter-horse farm in *Cleveland?*"

"Yup."

"Are you sure?"

"Yup."

Wes wouldn't lie about that.

In fact, as far as Carson could tell, Wes hadn't lied to him about one single thing, not as far as Carson knew, anyway.

He had no way to verify the Bad-Breath Pellets, Bullets, or Bombs.

Everything else seemed to be on the up-and-up.

Wes was a loudmouth, like Uncle Jim.

Wes had welcomed Carson. Even if he fell on top of him. He had invited him to his birthday party; he'd just forgotten to mention which month. He had made sure Carson had a number on a tongue stick. He had offered to sign his bingo card.

Wes had shared his lunch with Carson. And Carson had returned the favor.

So what if half of the half a *carne asada* burrito and six *buñuelos* went down the hatch.

Wes didn't share Carson's enthusiasm for rats. However, he had seen lots to love in Dandy, a crotchety old growly critter not considered very adoptable.

He had defended Moose when Cody made the wisecrack.

Wes slept next to a pillow with a rubber fish sitting on it, and so he and Carson had common ground.

As for the raucous romping, Wes was just being Wes. He was good at making long shots into the trash and could sound like a truck downshifting and honking its horn. That had to count for something.

One day he'd be out there with his nose painted red, keeping some young bull rider from getting trampled by a fifteen-hundred-pound bull.

"Let's you, me, Wes, Dollie, and the horse-face expert go on the trail ride. Deal?"

"Son?"

"Yes, Dad?"

"Loudmouth behavior like hollering, yelling, and shouting on a trail ride scares the horses."

"Oh."

"In other words, it's dangerous."

Carson was quiet.

"Okay, Dad. Then why don't we just go fishing? Patrick and his mom, Wes and his grandma, Nancy and her mom, you and me. Then we can go on a trail ride this summer, when Case and Gavin come up for a visit."

"Perfect."

"Except for . . ." Carson didn't need to finish the thought.

"Right. Well, Grandma and Grandpa will be coming up soon."

Carson's dad's cell phone rang in his pocket, and he checked to see who was calling. He went inside to answer it.

Through the screen door, Carson could hear him talking. "It's okay, Mom. Don't get upset. We understand, yes, completely."

He listened.

"And you know what? We feel the same way. Okay. Okay. Of course!"

He called, "Carson? Great news!"

He walked out and handed Carson the phone.

"Hello, sweetie! Grandma here."

"Oh, hi, Grandma!"

"Grandpa and I can't wait all the way till his vacation to see you, so we're just plain flying up for your birthday weekend. He's decided to take a couple of days off, the Friday before and the Monday after."

"He is? Great!"

"Here. Grandpa wants to say hi."

"Carson?"

"Hi, Grandpa."

"I'd like to meet that Mr. Nibblenose fellow. That was quite a good trick he pulled."

"Yup. A rat of many surprises. Can you bring up the croquet set?"

"On the plane?"

"I'm thinking maybe we can fish at the pond in the park and have a barbecue afterward and play croquet. Can you bring up your rod and tackle box?"

"Maybe so."

"Don't forget your fishing licenses."

"Roger. See you soon. Over and out."

"Over and out—no wait, Let me talk to Grandma again."

Carson whistled quietly until his grandma came back to the phone.

"Grandma? Do you think you could make a lasagna to bring to my class? And garlic bread?"

"Of course. But what about the You Gotta Be Kidding Me! Chocolate Calamity Cake?"

"Not allowed in school."

"You gotta be kidding me! No chocolate? What a calamity!"

"We can have it at the house, Grandma."

"Okay. I'll write *Happy Birthday, Carson* on top of the lasagna with melted mozzarella cheese for the school event."

Carson loved teasing his grandma. "Do you mind sharing the guest room with a few cute rats?"

"Of course not! Do I have to have them in bed with me?"

"Yup."

"All of them?"

"Yup."

"How many is a few?"

"Fifteen small and one medium."

"Fine."

Carson and his dad strolled onto the grass, with Genevieve romping behind them.

"So, after we go fishing with Wes and Dollie and Patrick and his mom and Nancy and her mom and Grandma and Grandpa at the pond," said Carson, "we'll have Shelly, Oswaldo, and Luciana over for tri-tip and calamity cake and a baby-rat shower. Okay? Also Eva, Matthew, and Zach. And Sydney and the Sporks Fairies. Can we set up a volleyball net?"

"Sure, why not."

"Good. We'll play croquet, play volleyball, and play with the pups. Shall we make a Birthday Prize in Disguise Surprise for Mama Nibblenose?"

"Of course. Is it her birthday?"

"It could be."

"Shall we make a birthday piñata out of a sock for her and fill it full of healthy treats?"

"Yes, most definitely."

"If it's warm, want to make her a wading pond with a paint-roller tray and put in frozen corn and peas so she can fish for 'em?"

"Yip."

"Can we make her a Templeton Trash Tub?"

"Tell me more."

"Put clean trash, like rags and wadded-up bags and newspaper, into a nice new plastic wastepaper basket, along with nuts, Cheerios, and yogurt drops."

"Sure."

"Shall we invite some more of the grown-ups to the barbecue? You could stand to meet some more people, Dad. There's got to be other fun things for you to do up here besides blogging about baked beans."

"I've been blogging about ranch beans, but yup. Let's invite the grown-ups."

It hadn't been easy moving before the end of the school year, from a very small private school where Carson knew everybody to a very huge public school where he knew nobody. It hadn't been easy, being the New Kid.

Carson had never been the New Kid before.

And it still wasn't easy. But it was getting easier.

Especially now that he had a few friends and a birthday plan.

"You're an awesome possum, Dad."

"You are, too. Happy Almost Birthday, son."

"Thanks, Dad. Can you speak Pig Latin?"

"A little. Not fluently."

"I think Dollie might be pretty good at it. Do you want me to see if she'll bring the LeSabre to the park and let us take it once around the block while everybody's fishing?"

"Aybemay. But rather than leave my post as host, I'd prefer to take it once around the racetrack. She has a pit pass, right?"

"Right."

It was fun being friends with Wes.

Carson's dad was right about horsing around on the trail ride, though.

Fishing in the pond with Weston Walker would be challenging enough, but at least a boat wasn't going to be involved. Dollie's Stink Eye had a better chance of working at the edge of a pond than behind a horse heading off into a ravine.

And they could sign each other's Hello Bingo cards in the "Went fishing" box.

•   •   •

Carson looked out across the neighborhood, above the treetops. Birds darted in the air, and landed in the treetops, and took off again. Above them, a hawk was catching an updraft.

Maybe it was Coop.

It was awesome having a pond only about a quarter of a mile away, as the crow flies.

Carson was definitely warming up to crows. If Bob crashed the birthday barbecue, so be it. If he got pushy about the tri-tip, Genevieve could bark at him and chase him away to roost beside his great horned owl gal pal with the pretty golden eyes. Sure, Genevieve was low-key, but when necessary she could get the job done.

Moose would hide under the covers.

As for putting him up on a shelf when Carson turned nine, forget it.

If there were life skills or guidelines related to the point at which a little old antlerless, wattleless, and cropped-tailed stuffed moose should be put up on a shelf, Carson didn't know what they were, and he didn't care what they were.

The day Moose would be put up on a shelf would

be the day Carson opened the door of his veterinary office. He would put him up on a shelf behind the counter beside a WELCOME sign and an artfully asymmetrical ceramic business-card holder that held a neat stack of cards that said *Carson Blum, DVM* in the middle and had a small picture of a moose jumping over the letters with his dewlap flying and his antlers grown back.

MAVIS JUKES is the award-winning author of several books for children and teenagers, including the picture books *No One Is Going to Nashville, Blackberries in the Dark, I'll See You in My Dreams, You're a Bear,* and the Newbery Honor Book *Like Jake and Me.* Other titles include several nonfiction books in a series for adolescents, the latest of which is *Be Healthy! It's a Girl Thing: Food, Fitness, and Feeling Great,* co-written with Lilian Cheung.

Mavis taught school for many years, then became a lawyer, before writing her first book for children. She recently returned to teaching full-time and is now a computer teacher in three public schools, teaching word processing, graphic design, and language arts to nine hundred enthusiastic students a week. It is from this job that she drew inspiration for the ideas and antics featured in *The New Kid.*

Mavis lives with her husband, the artist Robert Hudson, in Sonoma County, California. They share their small ranch with four cats, a dog, and numerous hawks, owls, raccoons, opossums, skunks, and other mysterious critters whose eyes twinkle in the dark. Mavis and Bob are the parents of four children, all artists.